Escaping from Hell

Uneven steps on the descending spiral

This is a work of fiction. Similarities to real people, places, or events are entirely coincidental.

ESCAPING FROM HELL

First edition. August 17, 2023.

Copyright © 2023 Francisco Angulo de Lafuente.

ISBN: 979-8223598688

Written by Francisco Angulo de Lafuente.

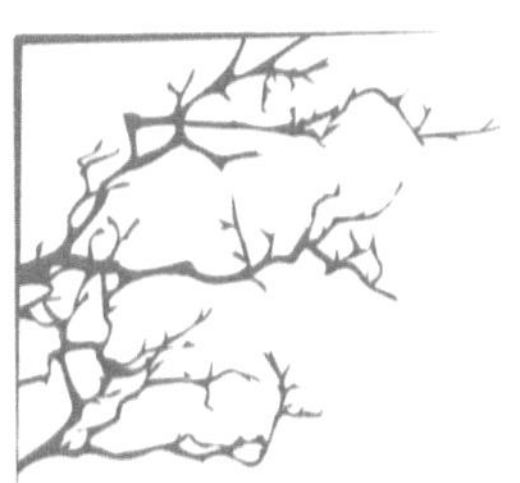

Foreword

Francisco Angulo's spellbinding novel Escapando del Infierno whisks readers away to 1930s Spain on the brink of civil war. Weaving together history and myth, this epic tale has earned praise as "an enthralling adventure" (The Times) with "breathtaking prose" (The Guardian).

Centered around Andrea, a courageous young archivist, and the mysterious Englishman Lord Edwards, Escapando del Infierno seamlessly blends thrilling action with poignant romance. Andrea becomes swept up in a nationwide hunt for an ancient text believed to hold magical powers. With Nazi forces also seeking the book, she and Edwards race against time to find it first in this "heart-pounding page-turner" (Booklist).

Angulo's vivid descriptions transport you directly into the chaos of pre-war Spain. The perilous road trips, evocative Spanish landscapes, and life-or-death showdowns will leave your pulse racing up to the satisfying conclusion. Critics call Escapando del Infierno "an intoxicating escape" (Kirkus) filled with "palpable romantic chemistry" between the two compelling protagonists (Publishers Weekly).

Building upon obscure legends and religious myths, Angulo has forged an entirely original story that stands out for its "incredible imagination" (Library Journal). This "unputdownable tale" (BookPage) will linger in your mind long after the final page. With its cinematic action, timeless themes, and poetic turns of phrase, Escapando del Infierno establishes Angulo as a shining new talent in historical fiction.

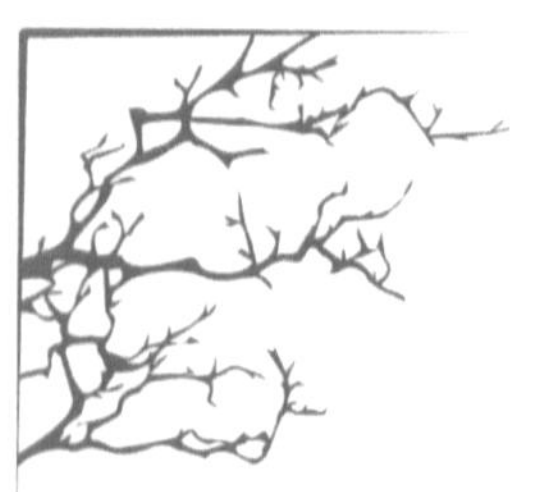

Prologue

Fish in an aquarium, ants in a terrarium or lab mice running through a maze. Our lives may be nothing more than that, a test to see if we find the cheese.

Doing nothing, the easiest solution, but in the end time pushes us to commit unjustifiable acts. Selfishness, fear, lack of empathy and the weight of the passing years. Ending up desiring the young wife of the neighbor, stealing the inheritance from siblings, falling into addiction to any drug that clouds our judgment.

Justifying the unjustifiable and moving forward on our knees, crawling or dragging ourselves like worms. You can't prepare for the race, pace your strength, when you don't know the distance; when you don't know where the finish line is.

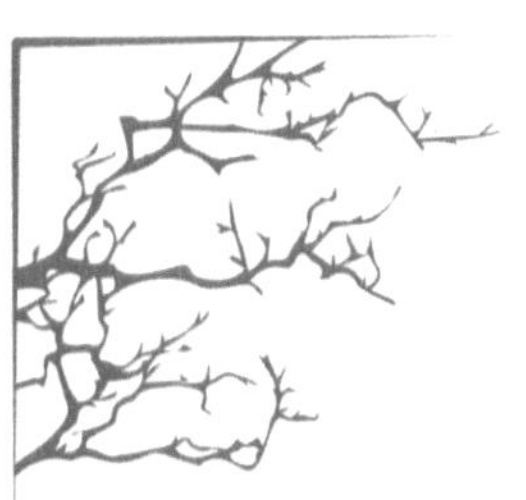

Chapter 1

Et incarnatus est de universo: tirra, aqua, vento et igni. Invoco deos inferos. Angeli de caelo et inferno. Vocem meam audi me et instruam te. Angeli atris profundis inferni. Eamque ponam custodes lucis. Sidera, terras et maria. Quod lux eorum qui onera portabant, et ignis flammae illuminare me.

The two young men uttered the conjuration in a trembling voice at the same time. They held in their hands an old book bound in dark brown leather, with covers worn by time. The bottom had a black strip, charred by fire, which in some pages had reached the margins of the text. Surely at some point in the past, they had tried to destroy it, but unfortunately or luckily something or someone saved it from the flames.

The two boys were in the center of a circle, to which smaller ones were joined at the ends, each with different symbols inside. They had made them following the instructions in the book: First marking the furrow with a walnut branch they had cut at dawn, just as the first rays of sunlight touched the tree. Then they poured a mixture of salt and charcoal onto the outlines. According to the text, the pentagram with its circles of salt and ash protected the summoners from demons. Before reading the book they didn't even imagine there was such a long list of fallen angels. They had to select the name of the devil to invoke, as different deals or agreements could be made with each one.

The light of the sunset with its reddish and orange colors bathed the old gray marble tombstones of the old cemetery. As they repeated the written words over and over, the wind suddenly ceased, an absolute calm took over and they knew they were being watched, the disconcerting sensation, the human-shaped silhouette they saw out of the corner of their eye walking among the tombs as they recited the invocation written in the book.

An anomalous gust of wind violently shook one of the cypress trees to the right, without anything else moving, not a leaf on the ground lifted and the rest of the trees remained still. The cemetery fully illuminated by the last rays of sunlight looked like an immobile oil painting on canvas, veiled only by the death throes of the cypress.

Inexplicable fear, terror suddenly paralyzed the two young men, who stopped pronouncing the confusing words. They had been preparing this for a long time and thought they were totally sure of what they were doing, but now it was as if they suddenly woke up, realizing this was no game.

- Did you see it? - Almost a whisper in the other's ear.

- Yes, there was something there, the silhouette cut in human form, walking among the tombs. - He pushed his shoulder against the other, scared to death.

- Take the branch and call him by name...

From among the hundreds of demons, apparently with different powers and ranks, in a strict military hierarchy, they selected one of lower rank to make the pact. In fact, both were atheists and did not believe in such things, so the main reason was to prove to themselves that it was all just old wives' tales. Having reached this hypothetical moment, there was no going back. The only way to safely exit the pentagram was to seal the pact with the devil first. The incubus they had invoked was a kind of treasurer, guardian of the underworld's riches. Once before him, they would have to negotiate the price of their souls and then one of them with the purified walnut branch would have to exit the pentagram, cross the gates of hell and touch the treasures with the tip of the stick before taking them in hand and returning with them.

Again total silence, as intense as if time itself had stopped. Now the light was so dim they could only see a few meters around them. The tense silence was broken by the snap of a branch, cautious, slow and hesitant footsteps were heard, as if someone was sneaking through the cemetery, then they were heard running closer. They closed their eyes in fear, if that diabolical being presented itself face to face, just two meters from the circular perimeter marked on the ground, they would die of a heart attack. Their hearts were racing wildly and neither dared open their eyes. They felt the presence a few meters away, heard it walk around the circle, as if examining it for a weakness, a crack to cross through. They could hear heavy breathing and a stench of rotting flesh reached them, similar to what they remembered when they found a dead dog on the roadside, which at first seemed to be moving and when they touched it with a stick its chest opened revealing thousands of worms devouring its entrails.

The boy holding the walnut branch in his hand, as agreed, was in charge of saying the final words and negotiating with the diabolical entity; But he was terrified, his heart was beating as if it would explode in his chest and he was breathing with difficulty, neither dared open their eyes.

- Come on, come on! - Said the other, elbowing him.

The words were heard several times repeated by that being watching them closely. The boy remembered a warning that appeared in the book: Demons could not be deceived, they are extremely intelligent and will always try to cheat before making a deal. They would try to cross the circle to attack the summoners or simply wait for them to leave the pentagram without the rod or sealing the pact. It also warned not to read the conjuration until protected inside the circle, not even read it quietly, because once the words are memorized, the devils will try to get you to pronounce them. With tricks and deceit, when you are asleep, they will whisper in your ear and make you believe you are inside the circle, so that between dreams you enunciate the words that open the gates of hell.

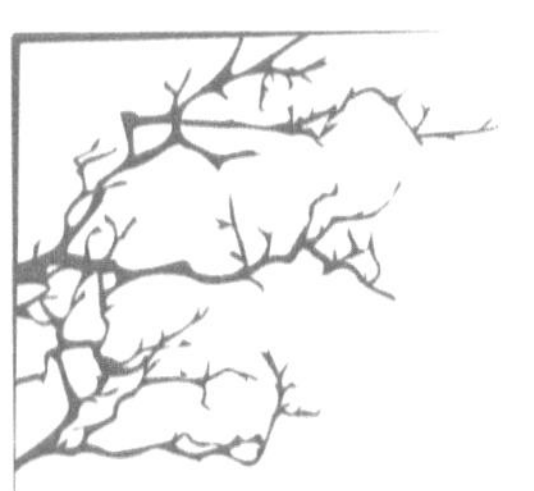

Chapter 2

In the summer of 1990, the two idle boys used to hang out in the old church square. It was one of the best places to take shelter from the scorching sun and high temperatures. There were benches lined up against the stone walls. In the north area there was shade almost all day. The square had been a garden up until relatively recently, now instead of grass there were whitish-gray tiles, with some crimson stripes crossing them forming larger geometric figures. Fortunately for those seeking shade on the hottest days of August, the old Salix Babylonica, weeping willows, remained in place, although they were not grouped or aligned, rather positioned casually, repeatedly breaking the new pavement's geometry. Thunderstruck by AC/DC played on the dual cassette deck radio, while one of the boys held up a hand with a pinned tape in a BIC pen, spinning it in circles rewinding it. The one holding the radio was a bit shorter, with black curly hair cut very short, almost shaved, brown eyes and tan skin. The other had long hair down to his shoulders, light brown, green eyes and surprisingly pale skin for that time of year.

They followed the rhythm of the music with slight head movements, when they heard the church door bolt unlocking, someone was opening it from the inside. Soon after, the priest, Don Ladislao, a tall, large, fat man came out. He approached them. With his white shirt unbuttoned halfway down, revealing his sweaty white tank top underneath.

- I like how this man plays guitar, although Paco de Lucía is much better. - He took out a crumpled handkerchief from his pants pocket and wiped the sweat from his forehead. - You have to turn the music down a bit, you woke me up from my nap.

The boy who had the music player on his lap immediately turned down the volume.

- Since I see you don't have much to do I'll propose a deal to you... - He placed his hand in a friendly, smiling manner on the shoulder of the one who was still rewinding the tape.

The two boys looked at each other, seeking some sign of approval from the other, they knew Don Ladislao's proposals were usually no fun.

- If you help me clean the square, I'll treat you to a Coke.

- Better some beers. - He immediately appealed, without stopping spinning the cassette tape.

The three got to work, the two young men equipped with broom and dustpan sweeping the square, while Don Ladislao gave instructions directing the operation. In just under an hour they finished the job and then the priest invited them into the church. Inside the temperature was pleasant, the stained glass windows illuminated the temple in multiple colors. They crossed through the central aisle, climbed onto the altar and behind it to the right there was a door that first led to a small room, the vestry, and then through another at the other end to the library, the dining room and finally the bedroom.

- Wait here, I'll go get the refreshments - He had said refreshments not beers, which worried the boys.

- Beers. - Replied the tallest one.

- Yes, yes, beers. - He confirmed with a smile.

The old library looked almost like a movie set, a cinematic backdrop. Totally unused, wasted place. With a huge rectangular wooden table in the center and twenty chairs on each side, which perhaps in the past had some use, with a conclave of priests sitting there or maybe a meeting of medieval knights. In any case it was inevitably sad, a depressing feeling to imagine the wasted potential of that place.

The boy with long light brown hair looked around the library in wonder. Ancient volumes bound in leather, with inscriptions engraved on the spine in French and Latin, there were some in Spanish, but those were the minority. The other one also came over to snoop around. Soon they looked at each other.

- Holy cow, this library must be worth a fortune.

- They must almost all be first editions...

- Crazy!

- Amazing!

Of course they were not experts on old books, but it was obvious that any collector would kill to own a library like that. From opposite ends they read some of the titles printed on the spines, passing their hands over them until they both met in the center of the room, looking at the same book without a title. They grabbed it at the same time.

- Here you go, nice cold beers! But don't tell your parents I gave you alcohol. - He had a mocking smile as he looked at the drinks, as if he had just told or done something funny.

He placed the three beers on the table, two pint glasses for them and a large white porcelain pitcher for himself. The simple comparison was insulting, showing the great and unjust inequality, but this time neither protested, they just took the glasses and took a swig.

- It's beer mixed with soda. - Surprised by the deception they looked to Don Ladislao for an explanation, while he laughed out loud. He laughed so hard he had to take out his handkerchief to dry his tears.

He took out a chess set along with a wooden box with the pieces, then dropped them onto the board and before asking if either of them knew how to play, he set up the game. The hand-carved wooden figurines looked like ancient relics.

- Do you play chess? - Asked the curly-haired brunette. The priest smiled crookedly.

- I was the youth champion. - He finished placing the last pieces. - What about two against one?

They accepted confidently, two young men against an old man didn't seem like a difficult challenge. They started the game, although the taller one couldn't stop glancing at the bookcase behind Don Ladislao, specifically, he couldn't stop looking at that unique untitled book.

- Are all those books yours? - He wasn't focusing on the game, although the priest played skillfully, without needing to stop and think about each move.

- They are old books from the church. - The other boy remained focused on the game, weighing the pros and cons of each move. - They aren't even from this one. They were moved here from some library or other during the war, the thing is they've been here since I was an altar boy and no one ever claimed them.

His curiosity grew. Lost books, older than the church they were in.

- And what are they about? - This time, before answering he made a quick move with the bishop.

- Check! - He smiled looking at them. - I haven't even read them. I think they're about religion, biblical subjects. Old stories and songs.

- Magic and spells?

- Don't tell me you still believe in magic? - He addressed both of them, but the other didn't even listen, focused on how to get out of check. - You can't believe in the three magi, people who fly or walk on water... and rise from the dead!

Don Ladislao kept flashing his smile, he seemed like a happy man, prone to worldly pleasures: good wine, beer and home cooking in rural restaurants. Hence his chubby figure, rosy cheeks and protruding belly.

- We don't believe in those things, you're the religious one. The one who believes in towers of Babel, Noah's ark and all those children's tales... - There were a few seconds of silence. Finally the other one moved, sacrificing the queen.

- No my son, don't get confused. - And he continued in a serious tone. - For me, this is a job like any other, they give me house, bread and wine... and what others believe doesn't bother me. Let everyone think what they want. As long as I stay warm, let people laugh.

- So you don't believe in God?

- I didn't say that. What I do or don't believe is none of your business. Priests, bishops and cardinals trip each other up to move up the church hierarchy. Those people believe in nothing but greed, blinded by power. Meanwhile, here I remain, priest of this old church. I owe it to my parishioners. And let each of them believe in whatever tales they want. - He stopped the conversation and made a quick move. - Checkmate, and now I'll bring you some real beers, you've earned them.

He placed the two glasses and empty pitcher on the tray and left the room, leaving the two young men alone again. The taller one got up and went to the bookcase, while the other kept looking at the board, trying to understand how he had lost the game.

He couldn't take his eyes off that mysterious book, he took it off the shelf and before opening it he carefully rubbed it with his hands, removing the dust. On the cover there was a spiral. Upon opening it he could see that the bottom of the pages were somewhat burned, but luckily it didn't damage the content, it had magnificent illustrations. Don Ladislao's heavy footsteps were heard approaching down the hall. Instead of putting the book back in its place, he hid it under his shirt, between the waistband of his shorts and his stomach.

- What are you doing? Have you gone crazy? - His friend was surprised, nervous about what he had just seen.

They were safe, sitting on the bed in the light brown haired, green eyed boy's room. He held the old book in his hands and they now examined it closely. Thick leather covers, smooth spine without inscriptions and a spiral engraved on the cover. It was very heavy for having three hundred pages. On the first of the two blank pages that formed the endpapers, someone had neatly written in pencil: "Andrea de Medina - Madrid 1936". That didn't mean anything to him. He turned the pages and stopped at the title: "Incantationibus est daemones ínferos." The letters resembled the negative of a photographic film, a kind of radiographic effect of the years and the ink oxidizing on the paper.

- You're taking Latin at school, right? - He looked while calling his attention with a slight nudge, shoulder to shoulder. - What does it say here?

The other took the book in his hands and brought it closer to see the words well. He pronounced them aloud, then thought for a few seconds, while his friend waited.

- Spells for the demons of hell. - They opened their eyes wide, surprised by the discovery.

They spontaneously jumped for joy, as if celebrating a goal scored by their soccer team. Then, without yet calming down, they fell silent looking at each other, thinking about the possibilities of that book. About the exciting contents they had left to uncover. Satanic incantations, a book saved from being burned at the stake.

The inside was full of diagrams, outlines and what looked like lists of names. Clearly the content had been translated into Latin from an older language, as some original notes or sentences could be seen that clearly did not match the text: marks similar to bird tracks, and others identical to Egyptian hieroglyphics.

- Well, can you translate it? - He took a while to answer, thoughtfully scratching his head as he scrutinized the book.

- It's going to be complicated, it will take me at least two weeks and I'm talking about the Latin part, the other stuff is impossible...

THE CEMETERY WAS POPULATED by ancient life-size statues of virgins and angels, the white stone had turned gray over time. From any carved area, dark streaks left by water fell, especially from the crevices of the eyes and mouth, making them even more creepy. They all seemed to be expectantly watching the boys who remained inside the pentagram. Many of the marble gravestone slabs had cracked over time, crumbling inward. On summer nights, the phosphorus and calcium from the bones produced a luminescent effect, causing some tombs to reverberate with a faint glow in yellowish and greenish tones.

The two remained with their eyes closed, scared to death, paralyzed, not daring to make any movement or say a word. The light brown haired boy finally pulled himself together. He mentally convinced himself that there could be nothing on the other side of the circle, since they had done all that precisely to prove that otherworldly beings, whether gods or demons, did not exist and never had. Before opening his eyes, he quickly dismantled one by one everything they thought they had seen or heard: It was easy to imagine human figures in the dark, even more so when the cemetery was full of statues, and the footsteps and voices could be noises produced by the wind, branches of the trees and even nocturnal birds, owls and screech owls. When he was convinced, he finally opened his eyes. He had closed them for so long and with such force that at first his vision was blurry. He rubbed them with his hands and looked around, everything was calm, he saw absolutely nothing out of the ordinary.

- You big scaredy-cat, open your eyes, there's nothing there!

- Yeah sure, my ass... - He resisted.

- There's nothing, damn it! - And he slapped him on the head with his hand.

Finally he opened his eyes and even with fear still in his body, he looked straight ahead, left and right. Once he saw there was nothing there he looked at the other, but at that very moment the same doubt crossed both their minds: Surrounded by darkness, they both realized they hadn't looked behind them. Before they could even turn their heads, a chill ran through their bodies, the hair on their arms standing on end. They heard noises, the clear sound of footsteps approaching. They immediately turned around and this time in the gloom they saw a human figure coming towards them.

- Scoundrels, get out of here, this is private property. - The guard shone his flashlight in the boys' faces and they ran out of the cemetery.

Chapter 3

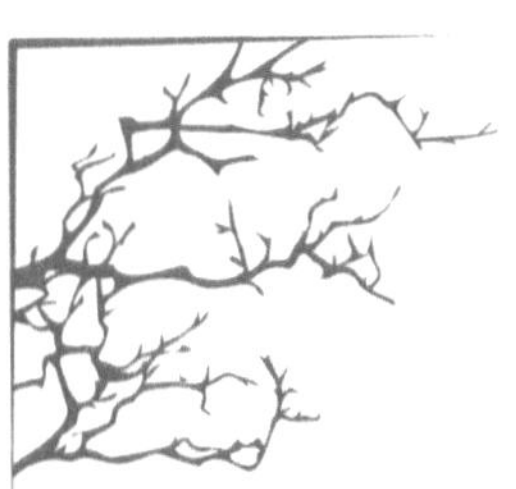

Recently, a large amount of material that had belonged to the church was made public and books with historical value were being cataloged to be kept in the National Library. That was Andrea de Medina's job. Her work consisted of classifying each of the copies that arrived, to later order them alphabetically by genre, title and author.

In addition to being intelligent and efficient at her job, Andrea was a very beautiful young woman, however she did not fit the canons of beauty at the time. In 1936 most men preferred plump women, who didn't ask too many questions and who took care of the house. They thought a woman's place was in the kitchen and seeing them outside of it bewildered them, they were a danger to society. Andrea de Medina, daughter of a famous architect, mother a teacher and writer of young adult novels, was the youngest of three siblings. Since she was a little girl she liked to wear pants and play with boys. She was a great horsewoman, but she also liked to play soccer, marbles and spinning tops, sometimes having to fight with the boys who tried to cheat or who after losing a bet, refused to hand over their marbles purely because of gender. They wouldn't accept losing to a woman. More than one, apart from losing, got a black eye. The boxing techniques her older brother taught her worked.

She wore a white blouse and cream colored tight pants at the waist. Her very light brown hair, almost blonde, was up in a bun, parted to one side with bangs falling over her right eyebrow. A lock on each side came loose from the hairdo, slithering down to her shoulders. Her eyebrows were light and finely shaped, naturally arched. She had a lively gaze, a bluish gray color and when she got nervous smiling, her left eye would shift slightly out of place. That involuntary gesture gave an image of fragility and made both men and women want to protect her.

That morning several huge wooden boxes had arrived, packed full of old books. Two deliverymen, aided by a cart, a wooden platform with four wheels, left the cargo in the warehouse. One of them handed her the paperwork so Andrea could sign the receipt. She put the pencil back over her ear and turned around looking for the exit.

She found herself face to face with the enormous box, she had already dealt with packaging like this before. Rough pine planks and long nails. Harder to open than a can without a can opener. Perhaps another woman would have sought male assistance, but she just needed to find a crowbar. After searching the warehouse she found one lying on the floor, covered by pieces of waxed kraft paper, left there by someone instead of cleaning it up after a previous shipment. She inserted the flat end into one of the top corners of the huge box and tried to pry open the lid, but her weight seemed insufficient to pull out the nails. She was in a somewhat comical position, with her whole body leaning on the iron bar, legs in the air to gain leverage.

- May I help you? - The gentle tone and distinctly British accent.

She then lost her balance in surprise and fell butt first against the box, the heavy steel lever clattering as it rolled across the floor. She looked at him with disdain, almost contempt, blaming him with her gaze for what had happened. He courteously held out his hand to help her up.

- Who the hell are you? - She was in a bad mood and angrily brushed the dust off her pant legs.

- I'm sorry, I'm very sorry... You should ask for help. - And he just stood there looking at her with a slight smile on his face, as if he found it amusing.

- No, I don't need anyone's help, I can fend for myself.

- Allow me to doubt that...

- Sarcasm? You lack manners... Mister, Sir or Lord or whatever. - It was clear from the extremely elegant way the gentleman dressed that he was no warehouse boy.

- Lord Edwards Llwch of Maiden, at your service.

- I knew it, just what I needed, a retrograde English Lord... - She was still angrily dusting off the front of her pants. - And now I would appreciate it if you left the way you came, as you can see I have a lot of work to do.

- I'm sorry to get off on the wrong foot, please let me help you. - And before she could even shake her head no, he had grabbed the crowbar and with a quick, skillful movement lifted the lid.

Silence fell, he stared into her eyes, flashing a gorgeous smile. That made her a bit nervous and her right eye shifted slightly towards the left one. Sensing that he had noticed, she blushed, a hint of color rising in her cheeks.

- Just luck, pure luck... - Edwards shrugged and now she seemed amused.

She held out her hand for him to shake it in a masculine greeting, he gently took it and as he slightly bent his knees, made a gesture as if to kiss it. She arched a skeptical eyebrow, as if dealing with someone not in their right mind. Manners and ways, far too proper and old-fashioned for such a young, handsome man.

- Andrea de Medina. - She finally said.

- Yes, I know, I was looking for you.

- I didn't know I was famous...

- You see, let me explain. I'm looking for a book and you can help me.

- Well you should look for it at the Cuesta de Moyano book stalls.

- On the other hand, your sarcasm doesn't make you seem ill-mannered. - This time they both laughed.

He began his story from the beginning: Sent by his country's Ministry of Culture, through the embassy, in a diplomatic capacity.

Searching for a book, which for reasons he did not reveal, seemed very important, since Nazi Germany's Hitler and Italy's fascist Benito Mussolini were also after it.

The Nazi SS were looking for it because they thought they could use it as a weapon, according to them it was a compendium of black magic spells, which could bring supernatural forces to their side. Demons of war, already summoned by the ancient Egyptians and Sumerians. Translated into Latin by one of Pontius Pilate's own scribes.

The British were interested in the diagrams that appeared, as they thought they could be used to decipher the encrypted messages the Germans sent by radio. The design of a device with rotating drums, that could decipher the messages from the Enigma machine.

On the other hand, the Italian military intelligence, who were simply trying to gain favor with the Nazis.

Father Sebastian, a very old, thin man, with ash-colored hair, wore a long black cassock that reached his feet. He spent the day working in the library, he was a historian and one of the most knowledgeable people in the world when it came to old books. He combined this with his ecclesiastical duties. On Sundays he still celebrated mass. Andrea thought that if anyone could know something about the book the Englishman was looking for, it would be him. She found him in a small room, under the light of a lamp illuminating an ancient manuscript. Wearing white gloves he carefully turned the pages, studying them in detail and taking notes in his notebook.

- Excuse me, Father Sebastian.

- Hello child. - He called her child affectionately. - Lots of work? Books just keep arriving...

- Yes, I don't know where we're going to put them all. - She looked at him, waiting for the right moment to get to the point.

- What do you need? - He winked at her. - You look prettier every day. If I were forty years younger, I'd think twice about joining the seminary...

He was a dear old man, cheerful and humorous. Despite his age, he had a lively gaze that recalled that of a child. Under the black cassock and wrinkled skin hid a lively young lad.

Andrea told him about the book, but he said he didn't know anything about it. He was very bad at lying, clearly deliberately hiding something. She didn't want to insist.

SHE GOT ON THE TRAM: The driver in a navy blue jacket and cap went about his business, without looking to see who got on, a middle-aged man who seemed to have been performing the same task his whole life. Precise, mechanical movements, like a Swiss watch, he could make the route with his eyes closed. The conductor was young and seemed more attentive to other things, girls who got on or walked along the street. The bell rang and it steadily accelerated, the warm, dry Madrid air caressing her face as she stood, holding onto one of the ceiling's leather straps, contemplating the wide street and buildings lined up on both sides immersed in the yellow and orange hues of dusk. All kinds of people from every social class could be seen walking along the sidewalks, refined people staying at the Ritz or Palace, groups of elegant businessmen in felt hats, impeccable couples, women in embroidered dresses, with long white gloves on the arms of gentlemen and also doormen at building entrances, clusters of cab drivers at their stands, smoking and chatting while awaiting customers and children playing, jumping over chalk geometric figures drawn on the ground.

She noticed a man who had gotten on at the same stop looking at her. At first she didn't pay much attention to him, but since they boarded the tram he hadn't stopped observing her surreptitiously. He was dressed completely in black, pants impeccably pressed with a center crease, vest and jacket, very short blonde hair, shaved at the temples and nape, slicked with pomade, combed to the right on top. Blond, blue eyes, young, tall and strong, well dressed but not elegant, his features were rough. Prominent cheekbones, occipital ridge and chin. All together it gave him a sinister thuggish air. A Nordic lumberjack in a borrowed suit and tie. You could tell by his forehead and hands.

The streetlamps lit up in unison. She got off near Sol and as she crossed the square, she noticed that man was following her. She quickened her pace, deftly dodging pedestrians, almost without turning around, from the corner of her eye she saw how her pursuer's bulky body stumbled over and over into people, nearly getting stuck in the crowd. Soon she lost him in the distance. She shortened her way home by going up Calle Carretas. Although the place tended to have prostitutes, it was also frequented by police. She looked back again, but found no trace of her stalker. A few steps up, there was a group of people, being pushed backwards by the nightsticks the police were using as a barrier held in both hands. The bulb of the lamp anchored to the wall illuminated an intensely red pool of blood on which lay a young woman on her back with a brutal gash across her neck, throat slit ear to ear. She had never seen so much blood before and it brought back memories of the slaughtering of a pig, its throat cut by a man in Ardales, a town in Málaga one March during the matanza festival. She still remembered the animal's shrieks as they slit its throat. So much human blood... and her knees trembled. She left the area as quickly as she could and shortly after, already at her building's entrance, wiped the cold sweat from her forehead with the back of her hand. She went up the winding staircase to the fourth floor using the banister, the elevator was still broken.

It wasn't exactly a luxury apartment, it was more like a small flat, bedroom, tiny dining room and miniature kitchen. All the windows faced an interior courtyard and at that hour no light came in. She flicked on the porcelain light switch, white circular switch and braided cord that went up the wall and continued along the ceiling to the bulb. The incandescent filament shattered the darkness, revealing the messy living room, all the books including the bookcase shelves strewn across the floor. The fright was greater when, upon looking up, she saw the man who had followed her, sitting comfortably reclined back in the armchair. Somber gaze and impassive face without any expressive features, holding a 9mm Parabellum Luger in his right hand, barrel pointed at the woman's face.

- Where do you keep it? - The grave voice, the German accent... - Where are you hiding them?

Andrea thought about the possibility of yelling for help or escaping, calculating each movement, reaction and consequence. She concluded that by the time someone came to her aid, the man would be long gone and they would find her dead on the floor.

- I don't know what you're talking about. - Then she thought those words seemed to be hiding something, as if refusing to cooperate. And she added. - I have nothing of value.

Now the face that had remained flat showed a look of dismay, as if he was used to people responding this way, making everything more complicated.

- Where is the book? - He stood up as he spoke.

That very morning this Lord Edwards had asked her to look for a book and also told her the Italians and Germans were after it. Now that spy novel-esque story was becoming frighteningly real. She thought she had nothing to hide, that telling the truth would get her out of the complicated situation unharmed.

- This morning an Englishman asked me about a book...

- We know. - He interrupted. And he said it in the plural, implying he was just the visible head. Behind, a long chain of command, SS officers, leading up to Lieutenant Hermann Göring and Adolf Hitler himself.

He slowly moved closer, stopping very near, their bodies almost touching. Andrea looked like a little doll next to him. He put the gun to her temple and with his other hand touched one of her breasts over the thin blouse, grabbing it completely. Then he slid his hand down her ruffled neckline, directly touching the soft, warm flesh of her firm breasts. She was scared to death, petrified. He brought his mouth to her neck and when his lips touched it, he removed his hand from her blouse and quickly brought it between the woman's legs. She didn't know where she found the strength, survival instinct perhaps. She gave him a shove and the gun fell to the floor, while he was still surprised, bending over to pick it up, Andrea ran to the terrace, went out on the balcony, but before she could even yell, he shook her violently from behind, throwing her off balance. When she fell she hit her head on the floor, stunned, blurred, cloudy vision. She had no way out.

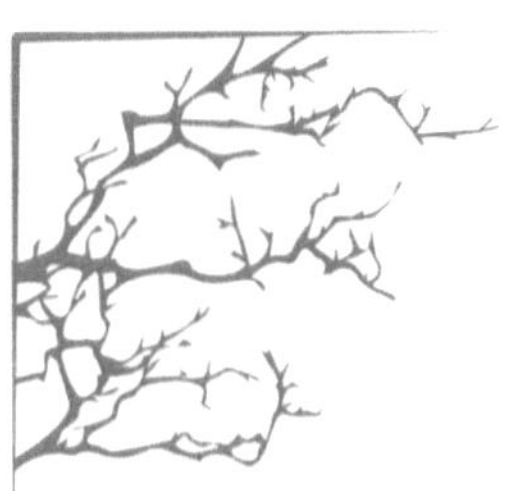

Chapter 4

After the elections on February 16, 1936 the leftist coalition, the so-called Popular Front, made up of an amalgam of parties: Republican Left, Communist Party, Spanish Socialist Workers' Party, etc. won the absolute majority.

After victory, some right-wing parties refused to accept defeat. Through different terrorist actions, they sought public support to overthrow the government. Attacks by radical far-right groups, such as those perpetrated by Falangists. The radical left-wing groups responded with vengeful violence by committing new attacks. In February, the criminal actions in repudiation of the government and economic situation had claimed hundreds of victims.

While chaos spread in the streets due to growing protests, high-ranking military officers conspired in the shadows, preparing a coup d'état.

On April 16, the murder of Andrés Sáenz de Heredia, a relative of José Antonio Primo de Rivera took place. The murder was carried out by an instructor of the socialist youth militias, one of José Castillo's men. In revenge, on July 12 José Castillo himself was murdered. This event led to revenge from the left, killing the next day the deputy José Calvo Sotelo, of Spanish Renovation. The death of the right-wing leader was the straw that broke the camel's back and those who had remained undecided so far finally supported the coup d'état. Taking the government by force and leading the country into military conflict. That was the atmosphere in the days leading up to the start of the civil war.

On July 10, 1936, the war was about to begin. First ours here in Spain, then in Europe and finally throughout the world. And he knew it, he could feel it.

THEY RANG THE BELL while banging loudly on the door. A man's inquisitional voice was heard:

- Police, open the door! - And he repeated it three times before Andrea could open it.

Her head ached and when she put her hand to the back of her neck she felt a bump. In the few steps from the terrace to the entrance, as she hurried to answer the police, she remembered what had happened. The books and shelves strewn across the floor, the open drawers and their contents rummaged through. The image of that man pointing the gun at her, the conversation about the book and what came after. She felt disgusted. She remembered the struggle, but what happened on the terrace she didn't recall clearly, the images were confusing. When he threw her to the ground she heard a terrifying sound, first lower and farther away, then the grunt or roar, as it reminded her of a lion's before attacking, was perceived very close by. The German turned and the light from the living room illuminated his face in an expression of terror. The next thing she remembered was the doorbell ringing and the severe headache when she got up.

She had barely opened the door when Lieutenant Martín's ID card peeked through the crack followed by his head. He entered without saying anything, observed the books scattered on the floor and without stopping for an instant continued to the balcony. He wore a rather wrinkled gray shirt, tucked into brown corduroy pants held at the waist by a black leather belt. The black leather shoes were very worn, if it wasn't for the credentials no one would say he was a police lieutenant, he looked more like someone who had just arrived in the city, with a cardboard suitcase in one hand and a chicken in the other. He looked around, seeming to take mental notes. Then he silently looked at her and after a while asked:

- What happened here?

At that moment she didn't know what to say, she just wanted everything to go back to normal, for that man to leave and leave her in peace.

- Nothing happened. - And she said it doubtfully.

- Well for nothing to have happened, I have a German down there who just discovered the law of gravity. - He motioned with a nod of his head toward the street.

When she leaned over the railing she could see the man's body, lying on the ground with dislocated, twisted arms and legs like those of a rag doll. There was also a large pool of blood, similar to that of the young woman she had seen murdered that same afternoon, only in this case, from a distance the blood didn't look as red. She noticed the feeling wasn't the same, seeing the stranger she felt pity, fear and anguish; The Nazi corpse gave her a certain sense of satisfaction.

The day dragged on, she hadn't slept a wink all night and luckily the police lieutenant seemed understanding, after asking her some questions, he decided it wasn't necessary to take her down to the station, although he warned her to make herself available, as he would summon her to testify as a witness. The excess coffee combined with tiredness produced a kind of flash when she closed her eyes. The bloody images of corpses in pools of blood and the feeling of panic when the man tried to rape her. She left the National Library before her shift ended, looking around as she went through the street door.

- Are you okay?

That voice and English accent were familiar. When she turned around she saw Mr. Edwards, smiling and impeccably dressed, neat as a pin. Andrea kept walking without stopping to say anything.

- I'm sorry about what happened. - She stopped short when she remembered, he came up to her and took her by the arm. - Are you okay?

A fleeting flash of terror crossed her absent eyes, then she regained her composure, stared at him fixedly.

- You've ruined my life. Stay away from me or I'll call the police.

- I'm sorry, it wasn't my fault. Had I not appeared, they would have contacted you sooner and you can already see what their manners are like... A war is coming and everything is about to start, here in Spain. That book can tip the scales one way or the other. - With a violent movement she pulled her arm free from his hand and kept walking toward the tram stop.

- I'm not interested in your wars... and I stopped believing in magic long ago... - The bluish gray color of her eyes was now lighter, like sunlight on a blue sky dispersing the morning mist.

He quickened his pace to catch up and walk beside the woman, she continued to ignore him. They stopped at the stop.

- Allow me to accompany you. - An automatic mechanism was triggered, but she held back her response.

In another situation, she wouldn't have let any man accompany her, as she knew how to fend for herself; but her recent memories, full of pools of blood, kept her silent, allowing the Englishman to accompany her. They both got on the tram and watched the streets and buildings bathed in the colors of dusk. Andrea eyed him out of the corner of her eye without him noticing. A handsome, elegant, extremely handsome man she thought. But it wasn't the right time, besides his old-fashioned style and manners, not to mention the fact he was a bit crazy. That's how he seemed with his excessive interest in an old book and that whole story. He turned and seemed to look at her amused, as if it were all part of a game, a dangerous game in which he had nothing to lose. Gambling with someone else's chips.

The café terraces were full of people enjoying drinks and the nice weather. He saw her look with interest at the all kinds of people sitting around the tables in folding wooden chairs. He pulled the cord that ran across the wagon ceiling from end to end, a bell rang and the stop light came on.

- Come on, let's get off, I'll buy you a coffee.

- It's not time for coffee. - Carefree look. - But I'll take a soft drink.

They sat on the terrace of the Círculo de Bellas Artes, on Calle Alcalá and while having a drink, watched people pass by.

- Where did you learn to speak Spanish?

- To tell you the truth, I wouldn't know. I travel a lot. I guess here and there. Books also help...

- Well you seem very young to have traveled so much.

- I'm not as young as I look and I've traveled more than you can imagine. - And he changed the subject. - Do you have two older brothers?

- Exactly. - She said, surprised. - How did you know?

- I was debating between two or three, it's obvious you weren't an only child, I can't picture you with braids playing with dolls.

- Actually soccer was more my thing... Does it show that much? - She smiled.

- I bet you still play better than most boys. - The comparison made them both laugh.

Now she noticed his iris green eyes like sprouts of grass and was somewhat overwhelmed by their bright, vivid color, which curiously she remembered as dull, inconsequential brown the day before. His face was angular yet at the same time beautiful, almost delicate and feminine, like that of a thin, athletic woman. Androgynous.

- Do you see the man in the gray pinstripe suit, with the straw hat? Turn without staring... - He motioned with his eyes to the right. - I saw him at the library door, he's been following us since then. And I think I know who he is or at least who he works for.

Once again nerves, the anguishing feeling of terror. Her nervous gaze shifted more frequently. She saw the man in the dark pinstriped suit: short, chubby and dark-skinned. Short, curly black hair. He didn't look anything like a spy either, he definitely didn't match the ones in novels or movies.

- He doesn't look like much. - The comment was spontaneous.

- Terenzio Nestore. - He said recalling the name. - A true fascist, he made a name for himself in the party by beating anyone who didn't subscribe to the Duce's ideals in the streets. From infantryman he rose to captain of the military police, but for that he had to torture a lot of people, men, women and young children, he had to rip out a lot of fingernails and teeth.

She felt as if her sweet dream was turning into a nightmare. The city and its people, which until yesterday had seemed peaceful and friendly, was now turning dark and gloomy. Until a few hours ago, she couldn't have even imagined there were people with such evil. Maybe a petty thief or an elegant white-collar criminal; but criminals and murderers she had only seen in fiction.

- Right there as you see him, he's more dangerous than an army of Germans. He can smile at you while stabbing you with a knife.

- You're scaring me... - She finished the soft drink. - Let's get out of here.

He signaled to the waiter and without asking for the check, left a bill on the table, enough to pay for what they'd had and several more rounds. A generous tip.

- Shall we get a taxi?

- I prefer to walk, I need some air.

Thousands of things went through her mind as they walked along the wide sidewalk of the Gran Vía. The streetlamps came on dimly, weakly.

- Maybe we should talk to the police. - She said pensively.

- I wish things were that simple. The police can do little in this matter, plus there are many sympathizers with the fascist cause. Things change, you must adapt. Most of these people. - He motioned ambiguously encompassing everything. - Are not aware that life as they've known it is over.

They walked a stretch in silence as Andrea turned the matter over in her mind. The word war kept hitting her over and over. These were troubled times throughout Europe, especially in Spain, but no one wanted to think about armed conflicts, the memory of the Great War was still very present in most people's minds.

- If I get you the book, will it all be over? You and the others will leave... - She argued, looking for a way out.

- It will all be over. - He repeated, for the first time truly serious.

- Okay, I'll help you find it.

They went down the slope to Sol square and then up Calle Carretas, she looked at the ground in the area where the young woman's corpse had lain and on the sidewalk she saw a dark stain left by the blood. He took her by the arm, forcing her to keep walking, to move away. She lived on Calle de La Cruz, next to Jacinto Benavente square. He accompanied her to the building's front door.

- Get some rest, we'll talk tomorrow. - He ended the sentence with a bow, like those performed in another era. He walked away down the street.

Going up the first steps of the staircase she felt the tiredness of the long day and sleepless night interspersed with short naps and startles. When she put the key in the lock she noticed the door was ajar, without turning the key she pushed and it opened. The fear that hadn't left her since the night before rose from the pit of her stomach to her head. The living room light was on. Upon opening the door completely, the hinges squeaked on the last stretch.

- Miss Andrea? - She recognized Lieutenant José Martín's voice. - Forgive me if I frightened you.

She found him in the living room, calmly looking at the books, as if he were in his own home. Now everything was tidy, each volume placed on the shelf in its place, arranged alphabetically. She had arranged them herself that morning before going to work. He took out a pack of cigarettes from his pocket and offered her one.

- Do you smoke? - She shook her head no. So he took out one of the cigarettes without a filter and put it in his mouth. He lit it with a match, without asking permission or whether he could smoke.

He took several intense drags, looking at the part of the cigarette that had been smoked between each one. He noticed the ash about to fall and looked at the rug under his feet, then quickly turned looking for an ashtray, but couldn't find one. Under the fixed gaze of the woman watching him, he flicked the ash onto an ornamental porcelain dish in the center of a round table. He barely noticed, he was thinking of more serious things. Of everything that had happened in the last few hours and whether it would be advisable to tell the policeman about it all. To tell him that whole absurd story about the book and the foreign spies chasing her. But before she could start talking, Lieutenant Martín spoke first.

- You see, I need to talk to you about something...

The unpleasant sound of the door opening was heard again and a short, chubby little man, Terenzio Nestore, appeared in the living room.

- I told you to stay downstairs, I'll take care of this... - And he ushered him out, practically shoving him.

The feeling of being trapped, like a goldfinch in a cage; It left her speechless, completely terrified. Then the policeman with the nearly burnt-out cigarette in his hand took one last drag and looking at her very seriously told her she had to accompany him to the police station. The German's case was getting complicated and he had to ask her more questions. He didn't quite trust the woman's reaction. He didn't want to cause a scandal in the neighborhood, hence he preferred to go to the station, although the Italian's intrusion revealed his hand.

She took a large off-white handbag and a wool jacket, as it was starting to get chilly out. They went down the stairs and in the dimly lit lobby, lit only by a distant yellow light bulb, Terenzio was waiting. He aggressively came up to the woman and shoved her in the back forcing her out of the lobby.

- Filthy communist!

Across the street was a black car, engine running and driver inside. At that moment the images of the young prostitute lying in the huge pool of blood came back to her head. And she was almost certain they were not headed to the police station, that if she got in that vehicle she would likely become just another dead girl in a pool of blood. She would show up in one of the crime pages of the newspapers, but no one would ask too many questions. A young, single woman living alone... Anything could be assumed.

The two men were behind her, the Italian fascist had his hand in his jacket pocket, possibly concealing a revolver. The driver of the vehicle with the black cap pulled down covering his face partially with the visor, leaned over onto the passenger seat, reaching for the door handle and throwing it open with a push, intending for them to get in quickly so he could leave there as soon as possible. Andrea looked back and forth but didn't see a soul, the area was deserted. When she was in the middle of the street, a Bentley Sedanca, which had been parked a few meters up, turned on its large, powerful headlights, blinding them. It immediately accelerated, its tires violently skidding on the cobblestone pavement. The winged emblem on the hood in the center of the grille pointed directly at the Italian Terenzio Nestore and approached at such speed that the two men had to jump back to avoid being run over. The British car's steering wheel was on the right side, near the two men who fell to the ground. The woman was next to the other door, it took her a few seconds to react, confused, until she identified the driver.

- Get in, hurry! - Said Edwards Llwch of Maiden, looking at the men who were already getting up.

Andrea got in as fast as she could. The car engine roared, the Englishman kept his foot on the accelerator and clutch, keeping the engine revving high so they could shoot off as soon as she was aboard. The driver with his cap was looking for something in the glove compartment, and instantly pulled out a revolver. On the other side the Italian took a small chrome pistol from his pocket which shone under the streetlights. The Bentley sped away leaving white smoke and burning rubber smell behind.

- Get down! - He shielded her with his left arm, catching a glimpse of the armed men in the rearview mirror.

Three shots were heard, one of them hit the cream colored top. The projectile forcibly entered the interior, impacting the driver's seatback. Andrea could see the hole it made in the dark brown leather. The bullet's trajectory went straight to Edwards' spine.

- Oh my God! Did they hit you? - She was very nervous. - Are you okay?

- Don't worry, it didn't hit me, the seat stopped it. - After checking the rearview mirror and seeing the danger had passed, he drove more calmly.

They zigzagged for a few minutes to make sure they weren't being followed. They remained silent, neither said a word until they reached the door of the Palace Hotel. The uniformed doorman greeted the Englishman by name.

- Please Felipe, take care of the car. - He handed over the keys again flashing his unperturbed smile.

The suite was larger than her apartment and equipped with all kinds of luxuries, very valuable furniture and paintings, all in a classic, elegant style. There was a low, solid wood table at the foot of an armchair with turned legs, upholstered in a light gray fabric with small floral motifs. Three or four meters behind was the bed, wide with lots of fluffy feather pillows. - A perfect bed for someone of nobility. - She thought. - Ideal for kings, queens or princesses.

They didn't talk about the book at that moment. They looked into each other's eyes in silence, hers bright, pearly blue and his increasingly green and luminous. He took off his jacket without taking his eyes off her, then the tie and finally the shirt, exposing his bare torso. He was stronger and more muscular than he appeared. In his elegant suits, he looked slender and frail, but his arms, chest and abs were those of an athlete. She wanted to caress his smooth, fair skin. Out of nerves again her right eye shifted on its own and seeing him look at her, she smiled stupidly somewhat embarrassed. He carefully placed the shirt, jacket and tie on the wooden valet. Then with his hand he pointed to the bed, Andrea grew even more nervous.

- You should rest. - And for the first time he didn't address her formally.

Without saying another word he turned toward the armchair, sat in it and took off his shoes, then lay on his side.

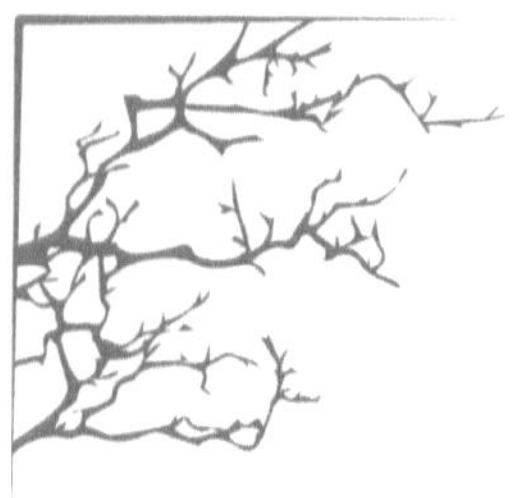

Chapter 5

The morning light filtered through the window panes muted by the thin silk curtains. She woke up for an instant disoriented, until she remembered what had happened, she felt energetic and hungry. She got up with wrinkled pants, having slept in them. She walked barefoot over the carpet without making any noise, until she saw Edwards' peaceful sleeping face on the sofa like a child's. No hint of worries to disturb him. Near the window was the jacket and shirt on the stand and almost in the middle of the back, she seemed to glimpse something. She approached in short steps, almost tiptoeing, to make the least noise and not wake him. Her mouth fell open when she saw the hole in the jacket. She put her finger through the fabric of the wool and inner lining, then almost nervously examined the shirt in the same area and was perplexed upon discovering the same hole. There was no wound on his back, no bloodstain on the white shirt... Maybe she should go over to the armchair and look at him again while he slept. She felt watched and when she turned around she found herself face to face with him, so close their lips almost touched. The green color now seemed deeper and was crossed by golden streaks, combining the very light brown star shape with the intense green outer ring.

- We have to get the book before they do. - He spoke as if he were one of those hypnotists who were in vogue at small traveling circuses and large theaters.

She instantly forgot about the mysterious tear in the clothes and thought again about the book, the aggressive face of the German who had almost raped her and his twisted, lifeless body shortly after. The dark-skinned Italian with black eyes and Police Lieutenant José Martín, who now despite his affable appearance, was the one who frightened her the most.

- I know how to find that book. - Pensive before speaking and then like someone solving a newspaper crossword puzzle, her face lit up. - In the Monastery of El Escorial, there is a kind of guide, a multi-volume register detailing the origin and current location where any church-related book can be found. Including those which until recently were considered forbidden.

THEY PARKED THE BENTLEY Sedanca next to the granite wall enclosing the monastery entrance square. The convertible top was down, it was a sunny morning and despite the circumstances they had enjoyed the drive. He was about to accompany her, but she told him it would be best if he waited outside. He could take a walk in the sun around the surroundings or cross the street and have coffee at the tavern across from them.

She crossed the front courtyard walking on the two-tone stone floor that forms a huge grid. As she approached the door, it seemed to grow bigger. The facade was full of rectangular windows, in addition to being a monument it was conceived by Philip II as a functional building, royal residence and monastery founded by monks of the Order of Saint Jerome. The monastery of San Lorenzo de El Escorial currently houses friars of the Order of Saint Augustine. She didn't have any official documents or letters, but trusted that with her ID card as a documentalist at the national registry, they would allow her access to the library.

She knocked on the door and after a while a small square hatch of about four inches opened, where the thin, wrinkled face of a friar with white hair and beard appeared. She repeatedly asked him to take her to the person in charge of the library, that it was official business, and showed him her ID. The old man was deafer than a post and she couldn't get him to understand anything. Rather than keep yelling, she showed her ID again while smiling kindly. The bolt sounded and the door opened, she followed the little man who suddenly on seeing him walk seemed rejuvenated, agile stride and rhythm, as if following the beat of a song, like a child on an excursion. He took her to the door of an office. He knocked with his knuckles, then opened it and with a courteous gesture invited her to enter, he remained outside and said goodbye with a wave of his hand while closing the door. Andrea looked around the dim room, the closed window and a single candle on the desk with stacked papers as if it were an office. There was a man with his back turned, drawing symbols all over the wall with a reed pen and inkwell. Now looking closely at the rest of the room, she noticed they were all painted with pentagrams, spirals, words and phrases in Latin. He wore the dark gray habit of the order, almost black, a long tunic, the hood pulled up covering his head and a white cord knotted at his waist. He kept working on his drawings, as if the woman wasn't there. She couldn't remember the proper way to address a monk, she hesitated between father or brother, so she decided to address him formally.

- Excuse me, I've come to take a look at the library's register.

- I know why you've come... - He turned around slowly. Sunken eyes of exhaustion ringed by dark circles, sickly white skin, withered from lack of sunlight.

She felt the sensation of fear again, of being trapped, similar to what she felt when she came face to face with the German. She held her breath for a moment and kept her composure. Then she spoke again in a calm voice.

- I need to find a book... - He fixed his unbalanced gaze on the woman's hands, as if he couldn't look her in the face. Then nervously, unable to prevent it, his eyes became fixed on a thick registry book on the table.

- It's no longer here... - And he changed the conversation to meaningless phrases and words. - No one escapes hell. The Antichrist has been reborn, the destroyer of worlds. The spiral is infinite. Death and destruction like the world has never known.

He seemed enraged or terrified, increasingly shouting, now pronouncing words in Latin. He grabbed a shiny metallic object that was on the desk, it was a sharp letter opener and when Andrea realized it, her legs trembled. The man was not even half the size of the German and she thought that gave her some chance. She calculated the time needed to reach the door and get out of there, but the distance between her and the disturbed friar was short, in all likelihood turning and running she would leave her back exposed to the dagger's sharp blade. She decided then that she had to use some kind of trick, buy time with an action that took him by surprise. She had already scanned the room for any object she could use as a weapon, but found nothing, there weren't even any chairs, just the desk with papers and documents, the bare walls soaked in ink. The flickering, dancing candle flame, nearly burnt out, cast long shadows that reached the ceiling. The man with his dark, sunken eyes and the threatening object in his hand, the tip pointing at her. She advanced her left foot and raised her hands, almost putting herself in a boxing defensive stance, as her brother had taught her. If the monk came closer, she would try to stop the attack with her left arm and then with her right hand throw an uppercut to his jaw, finishing with a left hook if necessary. Thinking like a boxer calmed her, removing the fear, concentrating solely on the fight, on each of their current positions and the following ones, on possible moves, attacks and defenses. Anticipating the opponent's movements like in a chess match. Silence fell, the man took a step forward, she vividly recalled her brother's voice, as if he were behind indicating what she should do: - Guard up, no tension, let him in...

He tightly gripped the knife in his hand, tensing the muscles in his arm, so forcefully it caused him spasms. He stared at her fixedly, his eyes wide open seeming to bulge out of their sockets. With a sudden, unexpected movement, he slit his own throat ear to ear. The bloody letter opener rolled across the floor and the metallic sound of it splattering blood overwhelmed her. Then the man fell abruptly to his knees, bringing his hands to his throat in confusion, as if unaware of what he had just done. Blood gushed between his fingers in spurts and a few seconds later he bled out, sprawled on the floor in the pool of blood. Andrea still unresponsive, thought that perhaps between the young prostitute who sold her body to survive and the friar who had isolated himself from the world in a monastery, there weren't big differences, at least not in the blood and manner of dying. The candle flame about to burn out sputtered struggling to keep burning. She quickly grabbed the registry book and hurried out. She crossed a hall, the long corridor and inner courtyard until she reached the entrance, the place where she expected to find the small, thin old man who had opened the door. But she didn't find anyone, and looking back and forth, everything seemed old and disused, as if that part of the monastery had been uninhabited for many years. Thinking about it gave her chills that ran through her whole body like an electric shock. The wooden door leading to the street now seemed rotten and had no bolt or knocker.

AT THAT VERY MOMENT, a beautiful twin-engine de Havilland DH.89 Dragon Rapide, with streamlined wings, coming from the United Kingdom, was about to land in the Canary Islands, to transport General Franco to Morocco. The plane took off from the London airport on July 11 at 7:10 am and stopped over in Bordeaux, Biarritz, Lisbon, Casablanca, Cape Juby. It picked up Franco on July 18 in Las Palmas de Gran Canaria and at 2:33 pm they left for Morocco. They stopped over in Agadir and Casablanca, landing in Tetouan on July 19, with Franco taking command of the nationalist troops.

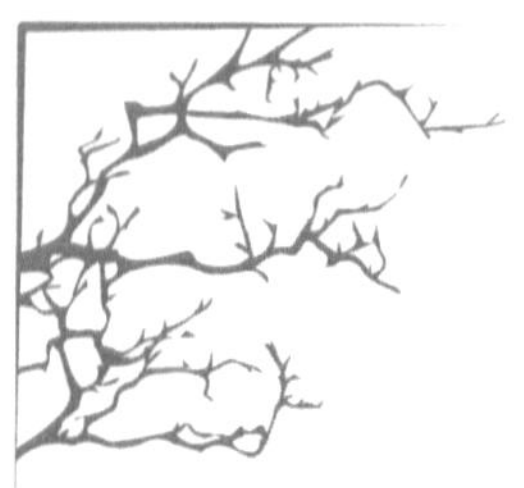

Chapter 6

The brand new Bentley Sedanca was parked in the same spot, but there was no sign of Edwards anywhere. She pulled the handle on the passenger side and the door opened. She sat with the thick book on her lap - it was quite hot so she left the door open - and began searching for any reference, but finding an untitled book didn't seem easy. The only thing she had was the description the Englishman had given her. An untitled book with a spiral engraved on the cover. She searched for references to engravings and spirals in books on black magic, but found nothing.

She had been waiting in the car for quite a while and her eyes were tired from reading the tiny handwritten notes. She closed the book for a moment and paused to think, what had happened at the monastery wouldn't leave her head and she was eager to leave that place. Over and over the man's shouted, almost screamed, words reverberated in her memory before slitting his own throat. The apocalyptic phrases and Latin words unknown to her, although she was able to identify some of them, such as hell, devil and end of times. It was possible that among those words or in the brief conversation they'd had there was some answer, some clue as to how to find the book. But she had the feeling that it had all been an attempt to conceal it, even going so far as to commit suicide before saying a word. Although remembering it caused her anguish, she went over point by point every word, every gesture and movement, like the autopsy performed after a chess match. When the friar turned fixing his sunken eyes on her, she asked about the book and then in a reflexive, involuntary act he glanced at the registry he had on the table.

- It's no longer here... - Those were his exact words.

She opened the registry at that moment, with renewed interest, as if now she had the key to deciphering it. She smiled upon confirming that page numbers appeared in the margins, the entry and exit dates of each copy. Among the last ones produced that same week was an untitled book, with a numeric reference.

Her hair began to stand on end as if her whole body was becoming electrically charged and she felt once again the sensation of being watched naked. That was not the right description. The feeling of being transparent, similar to what one can feel under an x-ray machine, or a psychoanalyst's watchful gaze.

- Do you have it? - He said very close by, startling her.

- Can you stop doing that?

- I don't understand: What is it I've done? - He smiled amused again.

- Never mind, forget it. - Her expression was one of resignation, as if no man or Englishman could be fixed. - The only thing that appears in the registry is a numeric reference.

She pointed with her index finger - very short but well-manicured nails - on the page under the numbers written in ink. He looked closely and became pensive. She closed it before his eyes, but kept looking at it curiously.

- They let you take the monastery's registry? - He seemed surprised.

Andrea was silent for a couple seconds. She didn't want to recall what had happened again.

- More or less...

- I thought the church was more jealous about their things, you know... You didn't steal it, did you?

- I think that's of little importance now, the best thing is for us to get out of here as soon as possible.

He got in the car without asking any more questions, ready to return to the hotel. While backing up to get on the road, in the rearview mirror he saw a car that looked familiar to him. The dark blue, almost black Citroën AC4 suddenly hit the brakes trying to block their path. Then he made out the driver, Police Lieutenant José Martín, accompanied in the passenger seat by the Italian Terenzio Nestore. They had positioned the vehicle in such a way that they couldn't get out onto the road. He then accelerated into first gear, the Bentley sputtered as its tires skidded spitting out the small white gravel stones that paved the surface. With this maneuver he managed to turn the car in the small space between the Citroën and the granite wall. Then he shifted into second and the car pulled onto the asphalt. The AC4 was no match, but the winding, sinuous road full of dangerous curves offered some opportunity; not to mention the possibility they might shoot at the slightest chance. Most roads at that time started paved or cobbled from the city centers and as they got farther out, they deteriorated, in many cases becoming simple gravel tracks or dirt roads. Edwards was an expert driver, he quickly downshifted when entering curves, pushed the braking limit, took a clean line and shot out, progressively accelerating. Despite this, the Citroën was catching up to them at times. The Italian with his pistol in hand, arm out the open window, forced the Englishman to make abrupt moves from one side of the lane to the other. It wasn't a fair competition. Shots were fired, but all missed. Andrea slid down in her seat to reduce her silhouette, at least this way she didn't expose her head. She held tightly onto the door handle with one hand and the side of the seat with the other. The vehicle continued bouncing and lurching over bumps, potholes and off-camber turns. Following the visual reference, José Martín was able to brake much later when entering a curve. At that point he got so close that on some occasions he managed to hit the Bentley's rear end, destabilizing it and almost sending it careening off the steep cliffs that opened up on the sides. Steep slopes where only some pine trees managed to take root. Andrea saw the depth of the ravines when the car skidded on the turns and went out to the very edge of the ditch. With some tires in the air over the precipice it wasn't hard to picture oneself at the bottom, dead amid a pile of scrap metal. With cool headedness, Edwards thought about how to get out of there in one piece. He gained as much speed as he could on the straightaway, assuming the risk that Terenzio might take aim. He precisely calculated down to the millimeter the acceleration and trajectory to enter the curve. He accelerated even more. He was going too fast and would be flung off the road by the nearly vertical slope on his right. He observed in the shaky rearview mirror that the policeman had taken the bait, flooring it following in his wake. The maneuver required all his skill, one hand on the wheel and the other on the gear shift. When entering the hairpin he slammed on the brakes, at the same time cranked the wheel to the inside, released the pedal, downshifted and stepped on it again, successively performing this operation until stopping the vehicle completely. Wheel, engine brake and braking interval producing an effect similar to what we know today as the German Antiblockiersystem or ABS system: anti-lock braking system. Lieutenant José Martín didn't have time to react and his Citroën AC4, sliding on the gravel with all four wheels locked, disappeared over the cliff leaving behind a cloud of dust and the terrified scream of the Italian Terenzio Nestore.

- CASA PACO - SAID THE large red letters on the entrance door of the white facade, then below in smaller print - Daily menu. They parked the lovely cream colored Bentley Sedanca with black fenders around back of the restaurant; Since they didn't know if there were more people looking for them. It was possible that by now there was more than one resentful German, Italian or fascist of any nationality. Out for revenge.

In addition to stopping to eat and regain strength, the exterior wooden posts leading to the establishment revealed the existence of a telephone. Andrea needed to get in touch with her brother, so he could pick up a suitcase with clothes from their parents' house, what she needed to get by, it was obvious that going by her house was not a good idea. At least not for now, until the matter of that book everyone was so eager to find was resolved.

Behind the glass door a spacious, rectangular room opened directly, full of tables with their glasses and cups, waiting for lunchtime. At the back on the left was the L-shaped bar and slumped over it, leaning on his elbows was Paco, the owner. The spring that held the door slammed it shut, startling the bartender with the jolt. Andrea looked at the wall clock: 2:50 pm, a good time for lunch and she thought it strange there was no one there.

- Can you make us something to eat? - She said, while the drowsy bartender didn't seem to react. - The telephone?

- The kitchen is closed, but I can fix you up something. Are you from far away? Don't you know what's going on? - He repeatedly, strongly rubbed his face with one hand, over his eyes and eyebrows: that might be why he had no hair on them. - With the other hand he pointed to the back, where the phone was.

Andrea went to the device, while the Englishman kept talking with the owner.

- What happened? We don't know anything...

- Well, Little Franco has moved to Morocco and taken command of the troops there. There are rebels everywhere, in barracks and naval vessels. Things are looking bad. Of course you French don't care... - He put three small glasses on the bar and filled them with red wine from an unlabeled bottle. He took one of them and drank it in one gulp.

- Thank you, but we don't drink. Is the situation really that serious?

- Picture it. - He made a circular gesture with his hand, encompassing the empty room. - People don't leave their homes... Go ahead and drink the wine, it'll do you good, today's a good day to start drinking.

He refilled the glass and drank it again in one go, then corked the bottle, hammered the cork in by slapping it with his palm and left it on the bar. With slight swaying as if walking on a ship's deck, he went to the kitchen. Shortly after he reappeared with a potato omelet. He also placed a knife and two forks near the wine glasses he had served them.

After several attempts speaking with the operator, she finally got connected with her brother. She gave him instructions, things she needed, approximate time and place to meet. She couldn't talk much more, the lines seemed jammed and the call got cut off. She went back to the men, Edwards had placed two stools in front of the omelet plate and was politely standing waiting for the woman. Old manners, chivalrous ways, which were fading. Andrea was so hungry, she couldn't stop looking at the omelet. She went straight over, cut off a piece and stuffed her mouth. The two men watched her in silence, with long faces, as if they were at a wake.

- What's the matter? - She covered her still full mouth with her hand.

- It's started. - He said it as if confirming the expected.

- It's going to get messy... - The innkeeper chimed in, making an indeterminate face by wrinkling up his face.

He looked at the wine glasses he had served them. Both were untouched, a real waste. He took one in each hand and drank them in succession.

SUDDENLY EVERYONE SEEMED to have lost their minds. Some were prying up the cobblestones from the sidewalks and placing them in the streets forming barricades, others were distributing weapons to the population. Communist style posters and banners with slogans were visible everywhere:

"They shall not pass. Madrid does not surrender. Unity is strength. Together we will win".

Andrea arranged to meet her brother Ernesto de Medina that afternoon at the Church of San Nicolás. They parked the Bentley in the same square.

- I'll wait here, with all this commotion, I'd rather keep an eye on the car. - Every now and then a distant gunshot was heard. With the distribution of weapons, it could be anything, young people testing a rifle in a field or small groups of one party or another settling scores.

The Church of San Nicolás de Bari was one of the oldest in Madrid, already mentioned in the 1202 charter. In 1825 it was ceded to the congregation of the Third Order of the Servite Order. The interior was dimly lit and only one person could be seen at the back. It seemed as if they had left the building abandoned. As she walked toward the altar, the figure of the man became recognizable, it was her brother Ernesto de Medina. Standing, with a gray suitcase at his feet. Gray pants and white shirt. She ran to him and threw herself on him in an embrace.

- How are you little sister? - The affectionate, cheerful way, while looking her up and down, like someone checking a doll to make sure it has all its parts. - Dad and mom are very scared, they saw that thing with the German in the paper.

- Tell them not to worry, that I'm fine. I'll come by to see them soon. - She had a thousand things on her mind, but recounting what had happened and the mess she was involved in wouldn't help. Her parents were already older and there was no need to worry them further.

- Things are getting really ugly. I don't know how long it will take the government to stop the rebel military... Things just keep getting worse...

- You could see it coming, politicians do nothing but divide the people. Instead of making life easier for us, all they do is create conflict.

Everyone wants to rule. Picture it, even party comrades stab each other in the back. Some distributing land, others handing out positions at will. All believing themselves Robin Hood, taking from some to give to others and we know, he who divides and shares, keeps the biggest portion. Haven't you noticed, that even in the smallest village, there are two blacksmiths? One from each party, when theirs are in power he prospers, all the work is given to him and when it's the others' turn to govern he's left twiddling his thumbs. If a mayor makes any improvement to his village: a road, a bridge or puts in a fountain. When it's the other one's turn the first thing he does is tear it down.

They talked for a good while inside the deserted temple. The light coming through the stained glass was fading. So Andrea thought it would be best to leave. Spend a few days at a hotel and wait for things to calm down. Hopefully, things would return to normal. Although this time, it seemed that besides luck a miracle would be needed. She grabbed the suitcase by its wooden handle and upon lifting it a small engraved tile was uncovered right in the center of the church. It had a series of numbers separated by dashes. They didn't match any date, it seemed like a random series. She realized they were grouped the same way as the book's notation.

- Do you know what this is? - She pointed at it with the tip of her shoe.

- The church code... - Her brother answered, as if it was something everyone knew about.

- What code?

- The Vatican assigns a code, similar to postal codes or license plates. Each church or monastery has its own. They used to use them in accounting books, to know how much was collected in each place. A way to measure the devotion of the faithful... - He smiled wryly.

He snatched the suitcase from her hands and accompanied her to the car. Once again the Bentley was open top and the Englishman was out sightseeing somewhere. He tossed the suitcase onto the back seat and after giving his sister two kisses, asked if she wouldn't rather he accompany her.

- Erni, I already told you, it's a complicated matter, but I'm in good hands, the Englishman who works for his government is with me.

- Okay little sister, don't be too hard on him... - She fell silent pondering, remembering if at some point... maybe in the library... she had been a little harsh.

It was practically nighttime when a man approached them from across the square. Tall and slender, with a firm, confident gait. Andrea immediately recognized Edwards' figure.

- There he is. - She motioned with her gaze.

- Well, be very careful. - He made a modest gesture with his hand, waving to the Englishman as he walked away, slowly fading into the shadows until disappearing.

He got in the car without saying where he had come from. He may have called his embassy for information. At least that's what she imagined. For a while he remained silent, sitting pensively behind the wheel. She broke the silence:

- My brother just informed me that the Germans have created a special SS unit, the Ahnenerbe, specifically to search for the book. - She slowly inhaled and held her breath for a few seconds. - Things aren't looking good, it just keeps getting more complicated.

- We can't let the Nazis get their hands on it. - His now very green irises seemed to glow in the dark.

- I think I know what the numbers that appear in the registry mean. They might indicate where the book is.

- Well then what are we waiting for? Let's get going. - The cheerfulness returned to his face. - Miss Andrea, tell me which way to go.

She directed him Sol and then down Calle Alcalá, to later go up Paseo de La Castellana, toward the National Library and to keep going. They passed Colón, went up to Plaza de Lima and turned right onto

Concha Espina, stopping at Plaza del Sagrado Corazón de Jesús. At the top of the huge limestone obelisk was the bronze figure of Jesus. To get there, they had to maneuver around countless unforeseen events.

When getting out of the car Edwards looked up at the dimly lit statue, illuminated by the electric lights of the nearby streetlamps and those coming from the windows of nearby buildings.

Chus... Chus... Chus, you always watching the game from above, without getting your hands dirty... - He murmured through gritted teeth.

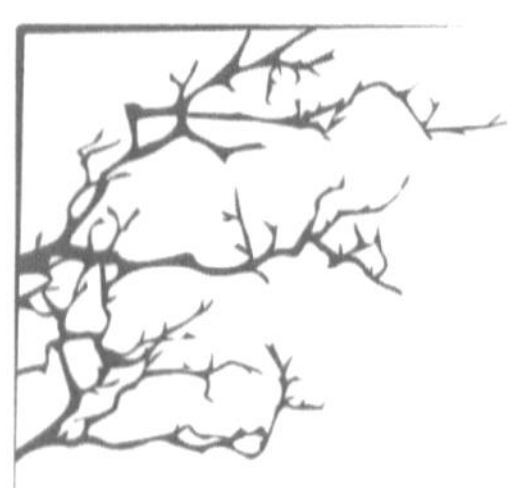

Chapter 7

The building's entrance was on the square, the doorman wasn't on duty. Disorder and chaos seemed to reign in the city.

Father Sebastian lived on the first floor, for work reasons, Andrea had visited him several times, almost frequently, to bring him urgent documents and reports that arrived at the library. Andrea knocked on the door, while Lord Edwards waited behind. At the second knock, the old man's voice responded and shortly after he opened the door. Father Sebastian wore a burgundy robe and slippers.

- Excuse me, I know it's late, but I need to urgently consult with you. Can we come in?

He opened the door all the way and stepping aside invited her in.

- We can? - He looked puzzled. - Are you with someone else?

He turned looking over his shoulder, just as he began introducing them. But when he turned around he saw no one there. Now she also looked bewildered.

- I'm sure he went back downstairs. These English care more about their cars than their wives...

Once in the living room, he invited her to sit. He had two comfortable armchairs in front of a small round coffee table. He went to the kitchen and came back with two glasses and a pitcher of lemonade. He filled both and drank half of his in one gulp.

- Well my girl, don't keep me in suspense, tell me what's going on.

- I have a numeric code, I think it belongs to a church and I thought you could help me. - Her hesitant voice as her mind went over what had happened.

- I imagine what this is about. - It was the first time Andrea had seen Father Sebastian so reserved. - It's about that book, isn't it?

ANDREA NODDED, THEN the old man began a long account and emphasized at the start the possibility that they were nothing more than legends and children's tales. The story began in Egypt's Amarna period. Akenaton fell in love with the most beautiful woman in the world, the young Nefertiti. But she didn't belong to royalty, her father Ay was a successful merchant who had prospered working for the pharaoh. They say Akenaton prayed and begged all his gods to be able to marry that woman. But none of them listened, so he renounced them, in the Valley of the Kings he invoked his father's and grandfather's gods one last time. Before him appeared the one who said he was his only God and granted him all his wishes in exchange for only praying to him. - Many say it was not actually God but the devil. - Everything seemed fine, Akenaton married Nefertiti, they stopped believing in the ancient gods and only worshiped one. They built a great city in his name, where the entire royal family moved. When happiness seemed complete, misfortunes began. Akenaton named himself god and granted Nefertiti the same power as the pharaoh, the first woman to have as much power as the pharaoh. So much time had passed since his pact that he had forgotten it. But the devil doesn't forget easily.

Plagues like the Black Death ravaged Amarna. Much of the population died, including several of the pharaohs' children. And the curse continued with his son Tutankhamun. The history, spells and pact were recorded on several scrolls. They say that was the origin of the book, some call it the black bible. Moses, one of Akenaton's best generals, was tasked with leaving with some of the survivors and taking the cursed book as far away from Egypt as possible. But it wasn't that simple, from the start there were conspirators, priests and generals who wanted to get their hands on the book. To use it to become pharaohs. One can almost imagine the rest of the story. The Ark of the Covenant. King Solomon, who they say reigned thanks to the book. It is said that the first Christians were actually the guardians of those writings. Descendants of Moses, brother of Akenaton, sons of King David. Persecuted by the Roman Empire, Pilate almost got ahold of the book, but no matter how much they tortured Jesus, they couldn't get a word out of him. Then the story becomes more diluted and confusing, it speaks of King Arthur and also recounts that the Knights Templar hid it in Spain. An untitled book, with the pharaoh's seal, a spiral, with which he signed the pact.

- Do you really believe that legend? - She asked incredulously.

- I neither believe nor disbelieve. - He finished the lemonade in one gulp. - The Bible also seems like a collection of children's tales, but new scientific evidence corroborating most of the scriptures keeps emerging every day, from the hands of reputable archaeologists.

Andrea fell silent, pondering the possibility that there was some truth to all that. Certainly the interest on the part of Germans, Italians and English gave pause for thought.

- Let me see that number. - He refilled his glass.

She handed him the last page of the registry book she had taken from the Monastery of El Escorial. She had torn it out and folded it several times carefully. She carried it in her pants pocket. Father Sebastian furrowed his brow in an unexpected look of surprise, he seemed to have identified where that page had come from. If she had brought the whole registry, he would have had a heart attack. He pondered for an instant after looking at the code.

- It seems familiar, let me confirm it. - He put on his reading glasses and went over to the large bookcase that completely covered the back wall.

He took a thick book full of numbers and names, similar to a phone book. It must have been some official church listing, which only priests had access to. He walked until stopping under the electric light of the bare bulb hanging in the center of the room.

- Here it is. - He pointed with his finger on the page. - Indeed, it's the Monastery of Montserrat.

A kind of whistle was heard, the bulb exploded plunging them into darkness. Then more buzzing and sounds of shattering glass. The window consisted of six glass panes framed in wood. Two of them had shattered and the fragments were scattered across the floor.

- Girl, girl! Get down, they're shooting at us! - He grabbed her arm and they crouched behind the armchairs.

It was possibly some sniper who didn't agree with the church. Maybe an anarchist or communist, some young man trying to gain favor and move up in the party. But it could also be Nazi or fascist spies. Father Sebastian told her to get out of there, that she would be safer anywhere else. It was the beginning of purges and score settling, what was called the paseíllo. Both sides would take anyone they didn't like out of their homes, under the pretext of taking them somewhere to talk...and then they shot them. No questions asked, no trial, judge or jury. There was all kinds, pure barbarism, if I don't like you I'll report you and they'll shoot you. In a town in León, a man hired two brothers as day laborers. They worked all summer scything, sickle in hand. Under the blazing sun, with only their straw hats for shade. When they finally finished the work and went to talk to the boss to get paid, he reported them, just so he wouldn't have to pay he accused them of being communists and a few hours later they were lying behind the cemetery wall, their white shirts full of bullet holes and stained with blood.

Below, inside the unlit entrance hall, Edwards waited sheltered against a wall, safe from the projectiles. The two of them waited a while for the right moment to escape from there and get in the car. The Englishman seemed calm, he took her hand, getting ready to run out. She shuddered. She felt his strong, warm, soft hands. His face profile and body silhouetted against the light. His scent of some kind of expensive London cologne she couldn't identify. The more time she spent with him, the more comfortable she felt, he seemed more and more handsome to her every moment. That's what she had noticed from the very start, he looked like a magazine model or even more, a charismatic Hollywood actor. For a moment she forgot about the situation, about the patiently waiting sniper. Without realizing it, she rested her right cheek on his chest, her forehead touched his neck. She listened to his heartbeat and wanted to stop time. It was just a few seconds, in an instant they were running to the car while bullets whistled over their heads.

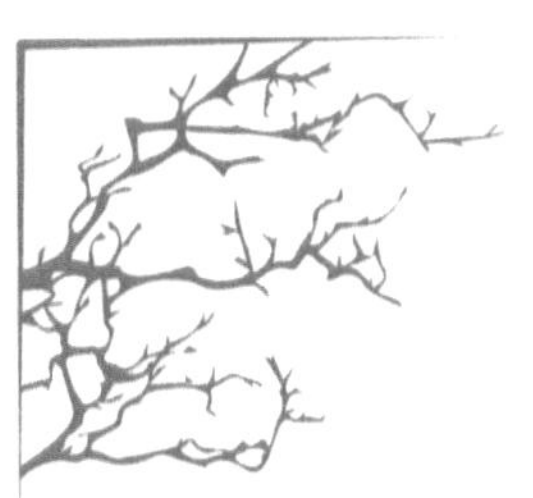

Chapter 8

On July 17, 1936, in light of signs of uprising, Giral ordered the immediate blockade of the Rif, sending navy cruisers and destroyers. On July 18 the Churruca went over to the rebel side transporting the first regular troops to the peninsula. But in Madrid, from the communications center in Ciudad Lineal, radio operator Benjamín Balboa, 3rd officer of the auxiliary corps, took control of communications, preventing the admiralty from transmitting Franco's instructions. Instead, he informed the vessels of the attempted coup. Once the troops were landed, the Churruca returned to republican hands. Thanks to said communication, the sailors mutinied against the officers, ensuring that most of the fleet remained loyal to the republic. The strait was secured, it was impossible to transfer troops from Africa to Spain. If General Franco didn't manage to transport his army, the coup was doomed to fail.

On July 29, Mussolini sent twelve Savoia-Marchetti S.81 bombers and a ship with twelve Fiat C.R.32 fighters along with their pilots and mechanics. To which were added the first twenty Junkers Ju sent by Hitler. On August 5 the so-called Convoy of Victory crossed the strait. With the bombers sent to transport troops, an airlift was set up from Morocco to the peninsula, transferring over 13,000 regulars and legionnaires from the African army.

CROSSING FROM MADRID to Barcelona, in a divided Spain, was going to be tricky, to say the least. Being English could indicate neutrality, but Andrea although she hadn't been a member of any party nor had any preference for one side or the other, by the mere fact of being Spanish and a Madrid resident, she could be taken prisoner by either nationalists or republicans. For any reason, it was enough for there to be someone with the same last name on the opposing side. Without needing to be family. There were checkpoints on the main roads, plus it wasn't safe to travel on them, as any vehicle was an easy target for aircraft. It took effort for them to leave Madrid skirting towns off the main roads. The dirt roads, besides being a challenge for the Bentley's suspension, often led nowhere. They could end at a farm or cultivated land. Edwards decided it would be safer to cross from town to town, on rural roads and paths. The journey would take several days, but better late than never. The first night he drove until late, then they stopped to rest for a few hours. Sleeping in the Bentley. On the front seats, which over time became uncomfortable. Andrea's legs were sore and numb from the bad posture. Upon waking at first light, she saw Edwards leaning over the map he had spread out on the hood of the car. He traced a route in pencil that seemed most suitable.

- How are you feeling? Were you able to rest? - He asked as he traced the route on the map.

- I have a hole in my stomach... I'm starving.

- There's a town with a gas station a few kilometers away, we'll stop to refuel and get some provisions.

- I'd kill for a coffee. - Her tone was amusing and he looked at her with a slight laugh.

THE MAIN ROAD CROSSED the town from end to end. They advanced along the northeast side, a dusty yellow clay road skirted it between the small stone houses with black slate roofs and nearby gardens. Not a soul was seen, doors and windows seemed boarded up. There were no gardeners working the land or shepherds with their flocks either. They stopped at the crossing that led to the back of the church, on the other side you could see a single story brick building, recently built, whose walls broke the architectural coherence of the area. Over the door a porcelain enamel metal sign read Ultramarinos in yellow letters on a dark blue background. To the left was a gas pump. Edwards parked next to it. They got out and headed to the store door. It was closed. He knocked with his knuckles and when he stopped an unsettling silence again took over. Andrea turned looking around. From where she stood she could see nearly a kilometer away, five hundred meters on either side of the road that crossed the town, from the entrance to the exit and there was no movement. The only living thing was the stork watching them from atop the bell tower. She tried knocking, hitting the door with her palm.

- Hello! Can you open up? - Her feminine voice was heard throughout the village.

Noise was heard inside, as if they were dragging heavy furniture blocking the door. A crack opened and just as Andrea flashed her best smile, the barrel of a shotgun poked out, aimed at her face.

- Get out of here! - It was a grave voice. - Right now!

A bald man, forehead to crown, with black curly hair in a strip ear to ear, with a thick mustache and sad small brown eyes that resembled an abandoned dog's. Andrea put her hand on the barrel and slowly lowered it, keeping her smile. Without fuel or food, they wouldn't get very far.

- We're just passing through, we've run out of gas... - Her gaze was clear, sincere like a child's.

He poked his head out into the street and looked back and forth, making sure there was no one there. He lowered the weapon and spoke as if afraid. He told them to make as little noise as possible and take the car around back. Following the instructions they drove around. The man was waiting for them with the garage doors open, gesturing quickly with his hands for them to drive the vehicle inside. Once they were in he closed it again. Now he seemed a bit calmer.

- The pump is empty. - He said as he slowly rubbed his bald head with his palm. - The anarchists confiscated the gasoline and left the store practically empty. In this town, we don't know anything about politics, we're all workers, what little we have we've earned through great effort. Now political commissars from both sides arrive to take everything. Without being from here or knowing us at all, they call us comrades, while robbing us of what little we have. If someone doesn't cooperate they get thrown on the truck, and are never heard from again...

He picked up two heavy cans he had next to the wall covered with a tarp. He placed a metal funnel in the tank opening and filled it with fuel. Edwards took a couple silver coins from his pocket and handed them to him with a grateful gesture. Then he said they needed some supplies. A door led to the kitchen. From the pantry he took chorizo, blood sausage and cecina. On one of the stoves he had a pot with boiling water to which he added a handful of coffee beans. The smell of freshly made coffee instantly spread. He wrapped the food in kraft paper and packaged it with an esparto grass rope. Once everything was ready, and before they left, he invited them for a coffee. The three drank in silence, exchanging knowing glances, as if they were the only human beings who still had some common sense left. The scene, the taste and intense smell of coffee was forever etched into Andrea's mind. The security of a burrow while outside the hunters with their dogs and shotguns lie in wait.

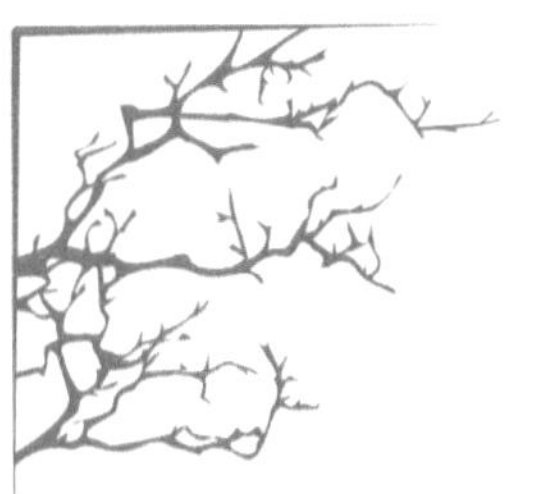

Chapter 9

The troops transferred from Africa to the peninsula, supported by artillery batteries, mechanized transport and aerial coverage offered by Italian and German bombers, began their advance northward. The brutality employed by legionnaires and Moroccan soldiers was devastating. During the taking of Almendralejo the Portuguese press reported over a thousand civilians murdered.

The African detachments led by Commander Juan Yagüe advanced unopposed, reaching Mérida on August 10, 1936 after traveling three hundred kilometers in under a week. After a battle lasting just a few hours, they managed to take the city. On August 11, the republican forces, made up of militiamen who had been expelled from the city, were reinforced by two thousand civil guard assault troops who arrived from Madrid. An attack was launched in an attempt to reconquer Mérida, but Lieutenant Colonel Tella's factions managed to contain them.

Commander Yagüe's army marched quickly to the city of Badajoz, which was under siege and defended by some eight thousand militiamen under the command of Ildefonso Puigdendolas. The first assault was carried out on August 14 by legion forces. The attack was repelled, the republican machine guns managed to keep the Francoist invaders at bay. The second attack managed to breach and penetrate into Badajoz's old town, although of the initial forces only a few legionnaires remained alive. The nationalist troops managed to advance street by street and by dusk they were already downtown. After taking the city came the bloody retaliation, known as the Badajoz massacre. It left the streets strewn with corpses. The killings continued in the days and weeks that followed, republicans who had fled across the border into Portugal were detained and handed over to the rebel military to be executed.

The rebel regiments in the north and south, where the July 18 uprising had succeeded, managed to reunify through the Extremadura campaign. Connecting the African army with the Northern army. The Battle of Badajoz in August 1936 put an end to the operation. After which the troops under Francisco Franco's command progressed swiftly through Extremadura.

IT WAS A VERY LONG day. Moving slowly along narrow paths and stopping every now and then to examine the terrain from atop the hills. When it started getting dark, they came upon a farmhouse with a hay barn. They parked the Bentley under an evergreen oak, next to the one meter high stone wall around the property. They jumped over to the other side and crossed the meadow already enveloped in the darkness of night. The structure was crude, crossed planks held together by nails. The door was closed. The Englishman pushed with all his might but couldn't get it open.

- Wait a minute. - she said, showing her palm.

She circled the building and climbed up the back until reaching a small opening that served as a window. She climbed up nimbly, holding firmly onto the wooden crossbeams. In an instant she was inside. She moved carefully not to trip on the farming tools. She removed the wooden bar holding the door shut, grabbed Edwards by the arm and pulled him inside. She barricaded the main door again and looked around. On a shelf on one side there was an oil lamp, with a box of matches next to it. The barn held tools for field work and in the back a pile of straw. From outside came the chirping of crickets and the distant hooting of a little owl. She told him to wait a moment and went back out toward the car. She returned with a wicker suitcase. Upon opening the lid, porcelain plates and cups were revealed, it was a picnic set that came as an accessory in the Bentley Sedanca's trunk. She spread a blanket on the floor, undid the leather straps holding the plates and cups. She sliced thin strips of cecina and placed them on a plate. Then she uncorked a bottle of red wine.

- I was saving it for a special occasion. - She winked and filled two teacups with the wine.

The two of them sitting across from each other on the red and black checkered blanket, enveloped in the flickering lamplight. Andrea completely forgot all her worries, as if only the two of them were awake that night, while the whole world disappeared. They toasted to the little things that make some moments special; Those rare moments that make life worth living.

Now under the warm, flickering light, he seemed even more handsome. His masculine, angular profile, pronounced chin and jawline. The two-day stubble, golden, coppery, orange tones, accentuated the shape of his lips. Andrea's eyes seemed bigger and lighter.

- Tell me about your homeland. Tell me what your childhood was like.

Edwards pondered for an instant, then began a narrative in the third person. Ambiguous, distant and impersonal, as if he weren't part of the story or rather, like someone recounting something that happened a very long time ago, so long that he no longer identified with it. The boy was born in an ancient city protected by four walls. In Maiden Castle. Although he belonged to royalty, his best friend was the son of one of the maids. The two went out every day to play in the surrounding area, catching frogs and insects. As they grew older, they ventured farther from the city. They went out hunting and exploring the territory. Sometimes they would ride for days. On one occasion, they reached a lush, ancient forest. They dismounted and tied their horses to a branch. They found the trail of a deer, which by the size of its hoofprints, must have been enormous. After following it for a while they finally glimpsed it in the distance in the depths of the forest. They split up, one advancing east and the other west, to perform a pincer maneuver. Llwch walked crouched among the lush undergrowth, carefully parting the branches blocking his path so as not to make any noise. The great stag grazed confidently, although from time to time it would stop, raise its head with its majestic antlers, turning it around, ears pricked and eyes wide open. To avoid being seen, he would lie down in the tall green grass holding his breath. When he finally got within shooting distance with one of his arrows, he stood in firing position, partially covered by the trunk of a birch tree. He drew his bow back with all his might, the arrow aimed straight at the animal's heart. He held his breath and just as his fingers were about to release the string, a young girl stepped in between, right in the line of fire. He managed to stop the shot in an almost miraculous way. Releasing tension by lowering it to the ground. She was the most beautiful girl he had ever seen. So gorgeous she didn't seem human, a forest fairy from a storybook. They looked into each other's eyes fixedly, when she saw Llwch lower his weapon she gifted him a dazzling smile. Time seemed to stop. The huge stag ran off and at that very instant, before the young man's enraptured gaze, an arrow flew by. His friend had fired before the lady appeared, right from the other side, but when the animal startled the shaft pierced the tender, white, soft flesh of the girl. She was still smiling without taking her eyes off him, while he held her dying in his arms. They did everything they could to remove the arrow and heal the wound, but it was very deep and wouldn't stop bleeding. Llwch placed the girl on his horse, in front of him, holding her in his arms, but he knew they wouldn't make it in time, as they were over a day's distance away.

- I need your mount. - And he took hold of his friend's horse's reins. - I'll send for you... Will you be alright?

- Hurry, don't worry, of course I'll be fine. - He spurred Llwch's horse on with a sharp slap.

He rode as fast as he could, while feeling her delicate body, growing weaker and weaker in his arms. The journey seemed endless, he crossed forests, meadows and streams, fast as the wind, almost flying at ground level. Every so often he would switch mounts to keep the horse from dying of exhaustion. It was nighttime already, she was unconscious and her body was turning cold, he placed his chest over her back embracing her and giving her warmth. He looked at the black, transparent sky illuminated by millions of stars and begged God to save her. At last he arrived in Maiden and his father's doctor tended to the girl, who by then was no longer breathing and her heartbeat could not be heard. But that doctor was no ordinary physician, he was so skilled at his craft that he achieved near miracles and thus, many people considered him a sorcerer or wizard. The boy went every day to see her. She soon regained her strength and they took long walks around the city. They were both in love, but she hid a secret, she never spoke of her homeland or family. One day they saw troops, thousands of infantrymen and cavalrymen, stationed near the city walls. An emissary asked to meet with Llwch's father to parley. Then he said they were aware that Princess Uindä Seibra "White Shadow" was being held in Maiden Castle.

The king summoned his son Prince Llwch and the beautiful girl. Then she recounted that they had married her to a powerful king, much older than her, whom she did not know and was not in love with. She did not want to leave, she wished to marry Llwch. He wanted the same and would not let her go. The emissary said Uindä Seibra's parents had already promised her hand to the king and if they did not hand her over, it would be a grave offense, ending in a bloodbath. Llwch's father owed it to his people and could not allow any bloodshed, besides his troops could not confront the large army besieging them, Maiden city would be destroyed. He ordered the guard to escort and confine his son to his quarters, while the girl was handed over to her rightful betrothed. Once Uindä Seibra was in the hands of the powerful king, he ordered the city be reduced to ashes. For six days they withstood the invading forces, but the huge army besieging them crushed them. Llwch and his childhood friend defended the castle, first with their bows, striking down many enemies with their accurate arrows, then when they managed to breach the walls, in hand to hand combat, fighting with their swords. Everything was destroyed, all the inhabitants of Maiden were massacred, women and children. Bodies piled on pools of blood. The city along with its people had been erased from history. From under a pile of rubble an old man managed to emerge, dusty and dazed. He searched for any sign of life among the bloodless corpses. He stopped upon recognizing the young prince's face. He examined him and then carried him on one of the horses that had survived. He took him to the forest and in a cave, employed all his knowledge to try to save him. On the third day he emerged from the coma and two days later was able to stand and walk. During the days he spent in the cave, he couldn't stop thinking about her, his father, friend and the entire town of Maiden, his whole family massacred. Trying to find some way to free her. But how could he defeat an entire army? Still very weak, he mounted the horse, ready to leave on what would surely be his death. Just before departing, the old man's figure stepped in his path blocking him. He knew very well where Llwch was headed, he also knew it was a lost cause. He told him that there was a way, a means to summon certain demons to fight alongside him. To do so he had to obtain the key to hell and only someone pure of heart, for a noble cause could achieve it. He then set out for the ends of the earth determined to find it.

- And that is the story of my ancestors. - His melancholy gaze was lost in the oil lamp's flame.

- Did he succeed? Did he find it? - Andrea's eyes blazed with curiosity.

- He never returned home. They say he wandered the world looking for the key and when he finally found it, so much time had passed that he didn't even recognize his own reflection in a mirror. He had forgotten his homeland, the golden hair and bluish-gray eyes of that girl. Despite all the pain of loss, the sorrow in his heart, it never left him.

- It's a nice story, but very sad. - Her gaze remained illuminated. - A very sad tale.

- Over time the story seems like fiction and becomes a children's tale. Forgotten is the color of blood and mutilated bodies. Describing war as a noble, honorable, courageous act.

He took her hand, which seemed small in his, and stroked the back with his right hand. The touch of her skin was soft and warm. Andrea wanted to kiss him, but contradictory thoughts fought within her mind. Animal instinct, desire and upbringing, rules, norms. She slowly moved closer, glancing down at his lips. She felt insecure, leaned back slightly preventing them from touching. But the urge was so strong in an instant that she lunged at his mouth, kissing him intensely. Without stopping kissing her, he stroked the nape of her neck and the soft white skin of her neck, where he felt the pounding pulse of her racing heart. Andrea wanted, needed to feel the touch of his skin, the warmth of his body and she unbuttoned his shirt. The yellowish halo of light enveloped them in a bubble where they felt out of this world. Edwards finished taking off his shirt, then helped her out of her blouse. He stood still, gazing at the bare torso, the clear, luminous skin, she glanced down for an instant while removing the cream colored lace bra. He kissed her as he pressed his chest against hers in an embrace. They were startled by noise and voices outside. They hurriedly got dressed, but before buttoning his shirt, as Andrea was putting on her bra, the door burst open. The wooden bolt broken by the brute force of the four men pushing at once. They were armed with rifles and shotguns. They were quite young, the oldest couldn't have been more than twenty and he was the one leading the group. Two wore worn and patched wool pants, and white shirts with rolled up sleeves to the shoulders. The ringleader wore a worker's blue overalls and an armband embroidered with the initials F.A.I. All four wore old, worn esparto sandals. All sun-weathered skin, short curly hair and dark eyes. By their resemblance, some kind of family tie could be surmised, brothers or cousins. They went by their leaders' last names, the one giving orders had named himself Durruti, the others were Líster, Negrín and Azaña.

- Hands up! - Shouted the one calling himself Durruti, pointing his rifle at them. - We caught you in the act...

Now all four of them laughed. While the alleged anarchist frisked Edwards, two inspected the barn, making sure there was no one else there. Then the four listened to the Englishman's explanations. But they didn't take him seriously, when he said he was an embassy envoy they scoffed.

- I think what we have here are two fascists, an English landowner and a lady... a phalangist lady. If you were republicans you wouldn't be fleeing Madrid...

- Should we take 'em for a ride? - Asked the one named Líster eagerly, hoping for an affirmative answer.

- No, it's best we take them to town, hand them over to the defense committee.

- But we could test the weapons by shooting them...

- I said no. - He had to raise his voice so he'd give up on the idea and the three boys lowered their heads gloomily, as if having a toy snatched from their hands.

Andrea and Edwards went first, followed by the four boys. It was pitch black and they walked a trail across a flat pasture area. The rifle barrel poked Edwards' back, pushing him to keep walking. You could hear the three behind whispering something at first, but they gradually raised their voices louder and louder. On occasion, the one called Durruti had to turn and tell off his buddies to keep them quiet. They reached a road, further ahead you could see a bridge crossing the river. They continued debating whether or not it was advisable to execute the prisoners. Questioning the authority of whoever was in charge.

At that moment the discussion escalated, ending in them insulting each other. Criticizing the actions of each of their political parties. Four boys from the same town, surely the same family, each from a different party or organization. The communist derided the government and said the president of the republic was useless. This made the one calling himself Azaña snap. On the bridge they started shoving each other and making threats, guns and shotguns pointed at one another. Edwards roughly gauged the bridge's height and the water flow, but in the poor night visibility, he couldn't know the depth or if there were rocks jutting up from the bottom. Still, he concluded that regardless of how high the risk, it was better than staying to see if they could agree on executing them.

A shot was heard followed by voices, shouts and insults.

- You gonna shoot me, you little punk? - He threw his weapon to the ground and raised his fists. - If you've got balls, fight like a man.

In an instant all four were brawling with their fists. Edwards firmly grabbed Andrea's hand and pulled her along. They both jumped into the river, luckily not hitting any rocks. The water was freezing and swept them away at high speed. There was random shooting every which way, no bullets came close, the darkness enveloped them and the current quickly carried them off. He tried to hold on to Andrea, but the force of the water separated them. Before losing sight of her he told her to wait for him at the car, though at that moment he was fully focused on staying afloat and reaching the shore before drowning. Several kilometers downstream he finally managed to grab onto one of the shrubs along the riverbank. She was soaked and her limbs were numb, she walked through a wooded area trying to get her bearings, but it was impossible in the darkness. She found a path that seemed familiar, she moved forward unable to stop shivering, teeth chattering. Near the right bank she saw a stone wall and further ahead the parked Bentley Sedanca under some kermes oaks. As she got closer she unconsciously noticed the bullet hole in the top, she opened the driver's door and crawled inside, curled up, frozen stiff. When feeling returned to her hands, she got out and took dry clothes from her suitcase, she changed without making any noise and got back in the car. As she reclined against the seatback she noticed something, upon feeling around with her hand she discovered the bullet hole went straight through. The hole in the seat was so big she could stick her index finger all the way through from one side to the other. The punctured top, the seat and also Edwards' jacket and shirt, but no trace of the projectile, blood or any wound. She couldn't find a logical explanation. The door suddenly opened, for an instant she thought it might be one of the young militiamen, but soon the smiling face of the drenched Englishman appeared, chilled to the bone, and still smiling.

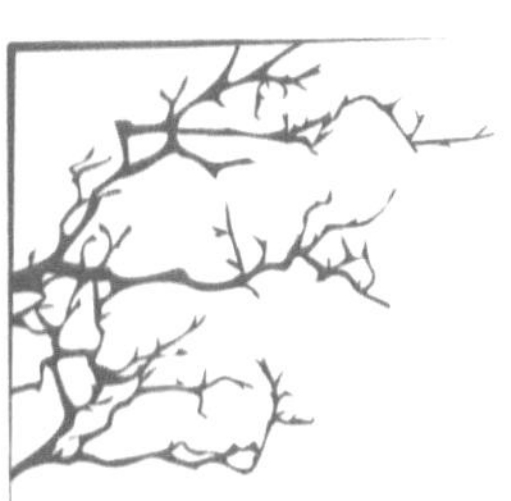

Chapter 10

They skirted Lleida, Mollerusa, Tárrega and Cervera, when the sun first peeked over the mountain peaks they reached Igualada. They were already at the foothills of the Montserrat mountain. Driving up to the monastery in broad daylight would have been suicidal. They hid it among some brambles and covered it with broom branches. Under different conditions the road would be beautiful, but fatigue was taking its toll. At times, Andrea's legs seemed like rags, unresponsive, and she frequently stumbled. Edwards held her by the arm, preventing her from ending up facedown on the ground more than once.

Legend has it that in 880 the image of the Virgin of Montserrat was found and the first four hermitages were built. Around 1025, Abbot Oliba of Ripoll and Bishop of Vic, due to the great devotion to the virgin that attracted large numbers of the faithful, decided to build the monastery over the hermitage of Santa Maria. The Romanesque church was built over the 12th and 13th centuries. The carving of the virgin venerated today also dates from this time. In the 19th century Napoleon's troops ransacked and set fire to the cloister on two occasions.

THE BACK OF THE MONASTERY is flanked by a natural rock formation, forming practically a wall.

- It'll be best to go up this way. - Edwards motioned to the granite slope, sliding his open hand through the air to indicate the route. - It's going to be tricky.

Andrea nodded, she was very tired and scrambling like a goat was the last thing she felt like doing at that moment. At some points they had to truly climb traversing, moving laterally. Fortunately they managed to pass between the two peaks, without needing to ascend too high, avoiding endangering their lives.

From the hillside you could see the unique structure. You could make out the old 9th century hermitage and then layer by layer like a Matryoshka doll, the Romanesque church and finally an austere building resembling a fortification, with a rectangular tower pierced by three rows of windows. Facing the square the building had four horseshoe arched doors and above them three large windows with balconies. When they came down to the square it was already past noon and the blazing sun at its zenith scorched. Hidden behind some bushes, they prepared to run across to the entrance arches. The wind was still, not a leaf stirred, nor was anyone seen or any sound heard. A gorgeous postcard. The stillness sent a chill down Andrea's back. She wore a short sleeve shirt, slightly damp on the back from the effort of crossing the pass, which increased the unpleasant sensation. The same impression she felt when leaving the Monastery of El Escorial; appeased only by the presence of the Englishman, who at no time had shown the slightest sign of fear or apprehension. As if sensing something, he looked at her with calm eyes, took her hand getting ready to cross the small square that separated them from the entrance together at a run. They ran as fast as they could, exhausted and sore legs, spurred by the fear of being a sniper's target. There were no shots or anything to disturb the deep silence. They caught their breath for a second on the other side of the arches, leaning against the stone wall.

- Well, where do we start? - Edwards' tired voice as he composed himself, hunched over, hands on knees.

- I'll request to see the abbot and tell him part of the story. - She placed the lock of hair sprouting from her temple, combing it to one side.

- What part?

- Yes, that's really the tricky part, telling the right amount. That you're sent from London, I'm in charge of the National Library and in El Escorial they told us the book was here.

They knocked on one of the doors and after the echo of the blows on the wood disappeared, the dreary silence returned. They tried once more with the same result.

- What do we do now? - The mix of tiredness and discouragement was palpable in Andrea's gaze.

For days she had been trying not to think too much, not overanalyze what was happening. People had gone completely insane, what seemed like a disagreement on the part of some military leaders with the current republican government, was becoming, in fact already was, a civil war. If the Englishman was right and that book could somehow help against the Nazis and Fascists, perhaps the military uprising would be quelled. Although the government had made many mistakes, democracy was always better than a military dictatorship.

- Let's move on to plan B. - He took a Swiss army knife from his pants pocket.

He fanned out its contents. The knife blade and instead of the typical tools, it had some flat prongs of varying thickness. He selected one of them and inserted it into the large, old forged iron lock, meant for huge brass keys, designed more to bolt the door preventing the wind from banging it, than to prevent thieves from entering. Two twists of the knife, the snap of the latch lifting and the door opened.

They entered the inner courtyard facing the front of the church. On each side rows of small windows with tiny balconies on four stories high. The monks' cells.

The church is accessed through an atrium where you find the 16th century tombs of Juan II de Ribagoza and Bernat II de Vilamarí, next to various sculptures. Saint John the Baptist, Saint Joseph and Saint Benedict. Also several paintings. The relief of Saint George heads the mural. Andrea stopped in the center of the circle, stepping on the words that read: "Nothing Comes Before the Love of Christ".

Several of the small doors to the Benedictine monks' rooms that opened onto the little balconies were ajar. The large wooden doors giving access to the chapel were also open. The uncomfortable, absolute silence continued, no movement or sign of human life.

- Hello, is anyone there? - She asked aloud, but no one answered. She turned looking at Edwards.

- We'd better go into the church, grab what we came for and get out of here as soon as possible.

That was the second or third time she'd seen him speak seriously. Andrea thought about what might have happened in that place. Whatever it was, they weren't interested in staying to find out. But she couldn't get the image of the slit-throat friar at the Monastery of El Escorial out of her mind. She had the feeling that upon entering a room or looking into a corner, she would find a pile of corpses, the bodies of those who until recently lived here. She tried not to think about it, to rid herself of the unpleasant images. She quickened her pace entering the church, immediately stopping to take in all the beauty.

The church is built in a single 68.32 meter long by 21.50 meter wide nave, with a height of 33.33 meters. Supported by central columns with carvings in wood by Josep Llimona, depicting the prophets Isaiah, Jeremiah, Ezekiel and Daniel. The main altar located in the central core, is decorated with enamels by Montserrat Mainar, depicting various biblical scenes: the Wedding at Cana, the Feeding of the Five Thousand, the Last Supper.

- Take a close look. - The Englishman pointed to the depiction of
the Last Supper. - They say it's an exact copy of an ancient painting in
the Vatican.

He then recited from memory the gospel:

When the hour came, Jesus took his place at the table with the apostles
and he said to them:
"I have eagerly desired to eat this Passover with you before I suffer.
For I tell you, I will not eat it again until it finds fulfillment in the
kingdom of God."
For one of you will betray me.

Matthew 22:15 - 22:17

- I don't see anything unusual. - She kept looking at each of the
figures depicted. Now with the words from the Bible in her head, the
apostles' gestures seemed to come alive. The commotion, confusion and
disbelief of one who looks with suspicion at who is beside him.

- Lower down, on the table.

Andrea's eyes opened wide upon finding a book with a spiral on
the cover near Jesus' right hand. It was substituting the classic chalice of
wine. The holy grail.

- Look at that one over there. He doesn't seem surprised, he's calm,
you might even say almost happy, staring right at the book, as if it
already belonged to him.

- Judas?

- Judas Iscariot. - He looked at his face, as one contemplates the
ravages of time on the face of someone not seen in many years. - The
thirty pieces of silver were an invention...

On the altar is the 16th century cross by Lorenzo Ghiberti. Above
it rises the octagonal dome. The presbytery holds paintings by various
artists. The two of them scrutinized the place looking for some clue.
Everything was just as it had been left, as if the people had simply
vanished. Right above the main altar you could see the virgin's camarin,
which can be accessed through the Puerta Angélica, an alabaster

doorway featuring sculptures of various biblical scenes, the work of Enric Monjo. Next is the Throne Room, decorated with a painting depicting Judith beheading Holofernes and Queen Esther's wedding to the Persian king Xerxes. Here you will find the Throne crafted in embossed silver and the 12th century carving of the virgin with angels holding the crown, scepter, and lily above it, all covered by a canopy.

- Let's leave the church, it'll be best to look in the abbot's office.

They entered the area where the monks had their small rooms. Plain white walls, only adorned with a crucifix. The beds seemed freshly made, they found no signs of violence. After going through the monastery, they finally found the office they were looking for. A small room, with a large solid wood desk, leaving barely any space to move around. On the table was an old black Bakelite telephone, with the handset off the hook next to a notepad with the first page violently torn out.

- It seems they were warned of something by phone... - Edwards muttered pensively aloud. - Maybe that's why they left in such a hurry.

- I wonder what happened here. - Andrea spoke as she searched the drawers, rummaging through documents.

Somehow, the Generalitat of Catalonia presided by Lluis Companys, had found out the book was in Montserrat. He ordered a group of civil guards to close down the monastery and take the monks along with the book to Barcelona. By the time they arrived there was no one left, the place was deserted, abandoned, all the monks had fled.

Abbot Antonio M. Marcet managed to escape to Italy, thanks to the French and Italian consuls. From there he tried to mediate to get the Montserrat monks out of the country. To get the book to safety, the monks dispersed into small groups, some heading north trying to cross into France and others south to cross the front lines and reach the Nationalist zone. Seven Benedictine monks took refuge in the monastery's residence in Barcelona, at 7 Ronda de San Pere. There they hoped the Vatican's intervention through the Abbot's mediation would send transport with safe passage allowing them to leave the country. At eleven at night, they were kidnapped by militiamen. They were dragged out of the apartment by force and kicked down to the street, without even respecting the most elderly. They were put into several cars and disappeared into the night's darkness. The next day, near the Pedralbes cross, the seven bodies appeared over a large blood stain.

Brother Bernat decided to travel alone and on foot. Thinking this way, he could go unnoticed among some of the refugees heading to the border. He crossed Gelida skirting it along the surrounding roads, without entering the town. He was arrested on the road between Gelida and Subirats. Seeing he didn't have the book on him, there weren't too many questions. He was slit throat right there.

Three other friars were murdered in the Can Campmany wells in Santa Creu d'Olorde. Monk Pere hid in an apartment in Barcelona, but was found out and taken to a cheka, in the San Elías prison, where he was tortured until they managed to find out the book had been sent to Toledo. After making him confess he was unceremoniously executed.

A small group tried to escape from Barcelona to Vic by train. At the station anarchist and communist militiamen stopped anyone they deemed suspicious. But the three Benedictines managed to board the train. The steam locomotive's whistle blew and with a jolt it started off. They breathed relieved, thinking the worst was behind them. But as if someone had pulled the emergency brake, the engine screeched to an abrupt halt, making the steel wheels squeal against the rails. A group of four young men from the FAI came towards them and made them get off the train. Their bodies arrived corpses at the Hospital Clínic. Due to their unrecognizable state and no one coming to claim them, they were thrown into a common grave at the Montjuïc cemetery.

The elderly monk in charge of the book chose little Tomasino, a ten year old orphan boy the friars had taken in. He sent him to Toledo, with a bundle on his back, bread and water for the trip, and the book hidden in a hem. With that and a blessing, he hoped providence would guide him to his destination.

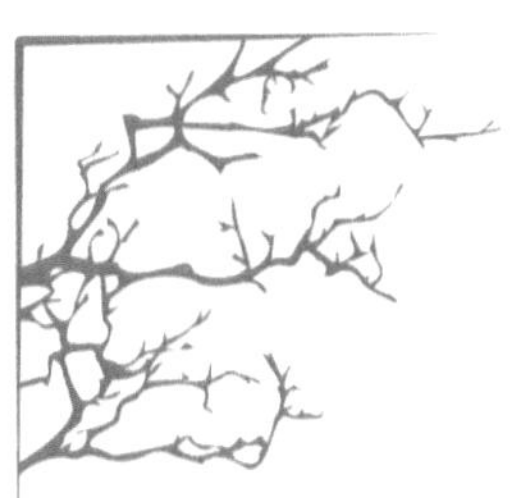

Chapter 11

Andrea had reviewed the notes, letters and documents from the abbot's office, looking for some clue, but she didn't find anything, not a hint of where the book was. The two of them remained silent, thinking. It seemed their path ended there.

"What do we do now?" She asked the Englishman.

"I'm sure we're missing something..."

"Well I didn't find anything, not even a mention in the letters written by the Abbot." - she looked pensively at the phone.

She picked it up and brought it to her ear, checking there was a dial tone. She kept thinking while he watched her absentmindedly. The rectangle of light coming in through the window shone on her hair producing crystalline highlights. She hung up the receiver and a second later picked it up again. She spoke with the operator to see if she could provide the last number dialed. She waited for the answer, pencil in hand, to jot down anything in the notepad. That was confidential information and she was not authorized to disclose it, was the response. While trying to wheedle something out, she made various meaningless scribbles on the paper. Upon looking at it, she realized something had appeared marked. With the pencil laid flat she smudged the area where words written on the torn out page had been impressed.

A distant hum was heard, increasing as it drew near. The roar of the three radial engines of a Junkers Ju 52. They looked out the window and saw a group of paratroopers jumping from the plane. A tactical jump with low altitude command opening, less than 1,200 feet. The round white silk canopies contrasted with the clear, blue sky. A unit from the SS. The Ahnenerbe, led by Heinrich Himmler, had been sent on a secret mission to Montserrat. Eight paratroopers landed in the entrance esplanade. Edwards and Andrea didn't have time to react, as they prepared to escape they were captured. A burst of gunfire barely missed their heads, the SS captain yelled at them in German, while the barrel of his MP40 submachine gun smoked. They raised their hands, she felt her legs tremble. Either side should have reported to their superiors, yet they took the law into their own hands. What could they expect from a group of Nazis who supposedly weren't even there? They could kill them at any moment and calmly walk away. Certainly wars are playgrounds for psychopathic killers. The more crimes you commit, the more medals they bestow upon you. The soldiers positioned themselves in a firing squad formation. Curiously none of them were blonde with blue eyes, Andrea thought absurdly. The captain gave a loud order and the squad aimed their automatic weapons. As they prepared to shoot, he spoke in Spanish.

"Where is the book?" - His accent was markedly German, his voice hoarse.

"We don't know what book you're talking about." - She responded spontaneously.

"I don't have time to be torturing you..." - A weary flourish, implying that if he did, he would have enjoyed it.

It was no relief, clearly he didn't seem to hold human life in high regard. Not having time to obtain the desired confession by smashing their faces with punches and ripping out their fingernails with pliers, only led them straight to the final point. He gave a new order, pointing at the woman with his hand. Two soldiers grabbed her by the arms putting her to one side, separated from Edwards. The group positioned themselves again in firing stance, this time aiming only at him.

"I'll count to three." - He showed an evil smile. - "Tell me where the book is or your friend will die."

There were no cards to play, the situation wouldn't allow it. What did she care if the book fell into fascist, Nazi, communist or anarchist hands? At that moment the only thing that really mattered was saving their lives. She hesitated a second: It was clear they had a lot of information, otherwise they wouldn't have made it to Montserrat. So telling a lie would be like pulling the trigger herself.

First she looked at Edwards for an instant, his face showed no fear, you might even say quite the opposite. It seemed characteristic of him. Whenever there was a really dangerous, imminent death situation, he didn't seem aware of it. Even more so, in each of those moments she remembered him as cheerful, almost smiling. Either he cared little for his life or there was something wrong with his mind. The second was pretty much evident. An English lord seeking adventures and fun, but the Germans' faces said something else entirely, for them this was no game. They stared at him intently, weapons aimed, index fingers tense on the triggers, ready to open fire on their captain's order.

"Toledo." - Andrea suddenly said, fixing her gaze on the nervous soldier's eyes.

"Toledo?" - He motioned to lower the submachine guns with a downward sweep of his hand. "Are you saying it's in Toledo?"

"Yes, the Benedictine monks sent it to Toledo. I swear that's all we know."

And now would be a fitting moment, given the location, to say they were in God's hands, or rather: in the hands of the Virgin of Montserrat. Two more bodies in the ditch, nobody cared, among so many corpses, so many mass graves and so many roadsides.

"Let's go, move it!" - The captain ordered at the same time he turned signaling towards the door with his MP40.

They crossed the atrium hands up, certain any sudden gesture would end in gunfire. The Germans' intention was to take the prisoners somewhere to lock them up securely, at least until they confirmed the Toledo lead. On the other side of the mountains, outside the wooded area, they had the extraction point. Two Fieseler Fi 156 Storch from the Luftwaffe capable of taking off and landing in a very short space would pick them up. Three paratrooper soldiers were up front, almost on the other side of the esplanade, where the vegetation began. Edwards and Andrea marched in the middle, hands raised. Gunshots were heard nearby and bullets whistled by much closer. But they weren't from the Nazis, they came from the other side. The two of them hit the ground, while the soldiers fired at will and ran for cover in the bushes. One of them was hit and collapsed dead on the spot. His lifeless body fell like a doll, violently slamming his face against the pavement, his head bounced on the cement.

She thought about making a run for it to get away from the gunfire. She lifted her head from the ground for a moment and looked at the Englishman asking him with her eyes what to do.

"Don't move, stay still." - Bullets buzzed over them.

The Republican militiamen advanced taking the square while the German soldiers had disappeared into the shrubs. A moment later the fighting ceased, communists and anarchists had taken the position. They argued loudly whether or not to go after the Nazis into the woods. One of them kicked the paratrooper lying on the ground, making sure he was really dead. Then he turned him over and thoroughly searched him, carefully sticking his hand into each pocket of his uniform without staining himself with blood. When those in command stopped arguing and calmed down, they came over to help Andrea get up. Both courteously, as if they'd never seen a woman before. While Edwards got up on his own, brushing the dust from his shirt and pants.

"Screw non-intervention policy." - His accent was deeply Andalusian. After examining the corpse he spat on it.

Dark skinned, with black, frizzy hair receding to the crown, broad sideburns. A rough, working class man, migrated from the countryside to the city. Around thirty something, with wide sideburns giving him the look of an old bandit.

"Corporal Baena, have some respect." - Said the one holding Andrea's hand, in a courteous gesture, signaling for the other to realize there was a lady present.

"My respects to the lady." - He performed an antiquated chivalrous bow mockingly, turned again to the Nazi and spat on him once more.

"You're so rude! Pay him no mind, miss, this one never even went to school..."

Surprisingly this time they treated them well, having rescued them from the Germans they even called Edwards "comrade". Of course, they couldn't just leave them there, they were obliged to take them to Barcelona and present them to the Generalitat. They were put in a ZIS-5, a truck made in Russia, that could barely make it up the hills. First gear and wheezing as if the engine would blow up. For now at least, nobody was pointing a gun at their heads, the conversation was relaxed and had veered towards British topics, talking to Edwards about food and sights. After much rocking they arrived at the city somewhat dizzy. Everyone seemed to be in a hurry to leave as soon as possible for their homes. So they went displacing the responsibility of taking charge of them, from higher to lower rank, with Corporal Baena ending up as the last one responsible. Had they been considered prisoners the treatment wouldn't have been the same. In this case, they were just a couple civilians the corporal had to take care of, play babysitter, find them something to eat and a place to spend the night. He was annoyed, he always got stuck with the dirty work. He took them to a boarding house, number 5 Carrer dels Escudellers, crossing the small Teatre square one of the narrow streets leading into La Rambla, from where you could see Columbus' statue in the distance. As in Madrid, they had torn up the stone cobblestones from some streets, then stacking them into small walls, improvised barricades, some even with canvas roofs set up like tents, chairs and tables inside where volunteers spent hours playing cards. On the walls there were communist style posters and banners with all kinds of slogans strung from one side of the street to the other. They entered the small doorway and went up to the first floor. The place didn't look too decent. And it wasn't. It was a brothel where Corporal Baena was a regular client. He spoke with the madam for her to give them food and lodging.

"How's the war in Spain going? We Catalonians have become independent..." - Corporal Baena talked as they sat at the table waiting for something to eat to be brought out.

After dinner of some lentils with hard crusty bread, the corporal went to a bedroom with María the Burgos Girl.

They waited a few minutes still seated at the table, lit by a carbide lamp which gave off a strong, unpleasant rotten egg smelling gas from inside. Andrea peeked into the hall, once she'd made sure no one was around, they left the brothel. When Corporal Baena was notified mid-act, he came out to the street in his underwear, but by then they were long gone. He shouted various profanities at the sky and with a look of resignation, went back upstairs, grabbed a bottle of anise liquor and drinking straight from it returned to bed with the Burgos Girl.

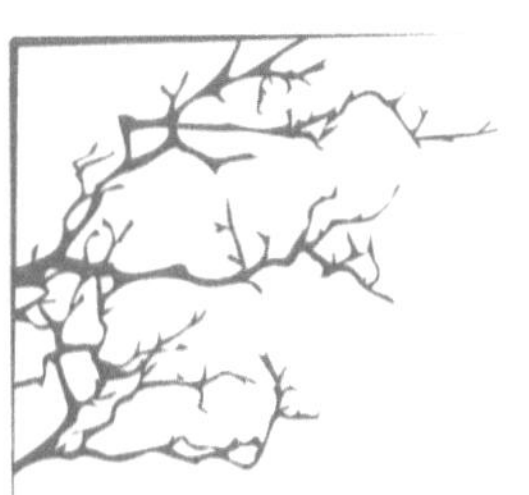

Chapter 12

Inside Barcelona the organization was anarchic and chaotic, many people in command and few following orders. Incredibly the city seemed to function, perhaps our society is not so complex, nor does it need intricate cogs, parts or springs. It functions the same without presidents, generals or monarchs. Protozoa in a pond, ants or bees; each one knows what they have to do.

It wasn't difficult for them to move around the city, but leaving was another story. All the roads in and out were watched. The checkpoints could only be crossed by showing a pass, every vehicle was searched. Getting out of there didn't seem simple and if they managed it, they didn't know how to travel to Toledo. Edwards thought about stealing a car, but after thinking it over he concluded the best would be to continue on foot, walking the coast southward. Abandon logic and common sense. In times of war, the longest road is often the fastest and the slowest transport the safest.

They went along the coast a few dozen kilometers inland. From the summit of some mountains they could make out a few coastal towns with the blue sea in the background. A distance opened between the small fishing and farming villages along the coast and others located further inland. Walking through no man's land, usually cutting across country, crossing pine forests and skirting steep, vertical rock formations. Stopping every so often, to make sure they didn't see or hear anyone nearby. In a few days their clothes were filthy and tattered and their faces marked by fatigue. They survived eating wild fruits and taking advantage of the darkness of night, sometimes breaking into an orchard to steal.

Andrea got up dizzy, she'd spent the whole day shivering. As always, Edwards was ready long ago, set to continue the march. She got to her feet, but her head was spinning and she fell to her knees, feeling the thin, dry pine needles prick her like needles. Then came the nausea, although she couldn't vomit, because despite the effort her stomach was completely empty. It was getting dark, they tried to move at the least busy hours and rested in caves or among brambles and bushes during the day. Despite her condition she insisted on pushing forward.

"Take it easy, rest a while, I'll go on ahead to take a look, see if I can find some food."

She curled up on the ground, under the pines, surrounded by bushes, drowsy, with her eyes closed but intermittent expressions of anguish and pain on her face. She woke up shortly after from dry heaves and upon finding herself alone as it grew dark she became afraid of dying there like a dog. Her sense of time was lost, minutes seemed like hours and hours like days. She felt as if the Englishman had left, abandoning her days or weeks ago.

Going down the hill covered in kermes oak he came to a small valley crossed by a stream. At the bottom you could see a small farmhouse. Its whitewashed walls seemed to glow under the moonlight. He headed for the back, where a small enclosure meant for holding goats and sheep seemed empty. Had there been sheepdogs, they would have detected him long before he approached, warning with their barking. No light was seen inside. He waited silently for a moment with his hands on the pine trunks forming the fence. At the back against the house, on the wall facing the north slope he thought he saw something moving in the shadows. Something was moving. He jumped inside and discovered a sort of cage made of wood and wire mesh holding some chickens. Some eggs and a roasted chicken would be ideal for Andrea to regain some strength. The small door was closed, tied with cord. When he went in there was a great commotion, the birds flapped around inside the small coop. Despite the limited space it was hard for him to catch one. As he opened the door to leave, chicken under his arm, the light from a flashlight shining in his eyes made him raise his other hand to shade them.

"Hands up thief!" - It was a hoarse voice, he couldn't make out the face, only the silhouette backlit. A broad, strong, rather short man. "Do we kill him or not kill him?"

Raising his hands, the chicken fell to the ground on its crouched legs, remained still for a few moments, then ran to the corner taking shelter with the rest.

"You see, I thought the house was abandoned."

"You take me for a fool?" - The tone seemed somewhat calmer. The English appearance and accent had him baffled. "Best we put a bullet in him right away."

"I know, it's not proper, but I have reasons for being driven to these extremes." - It didn't allow for making up false stories. Better to tell the truth.

"If your reason is hunger, you've got it wrong. Food is scarce everywhere and we don't plan on running a hospice. Who are you and where are you from? Nationalist or Republican?" - They kept the flashlight on Edwards' face and at times he spoke referring to himself in the plural. Perhaps living alone in that lost valley in the middle of nowhere had driven him a bit mad.

"I'm English, the war caught me by surprise, I'm not on any side. The reason for taking the chicken..."

"Stealing, you mean..." - The other interrupted.

"I'm traveling with a young girl who's very ill, we've been walking for days barely eating."

There was a new silence and after thinking it over for a few moments, the man decided to help them. He accompanied Edwards to where Andrea de Medina was. They found her curled up on the ground, semi-conscious. Claudio, the man who lived alone like a hermit in the small valley, placed his palm on her forehead.

"Poor girl... She has a high fever..." - Now Claudio seemed gentle and sensitive, like a bear caring for its cubs.

Between the two of them they brought her down from the hills and into the house, where Claudio laid her on his bed, then placed a damp cloth on her forehead and rummaged in a cupboard drawer where he kept medicinal herbs with which he prepared his own homemade remedies. Edwards spent the night at her side, silent, watchful. The next morning Andrea seemed out of danger, although she still felt very ill. She spent five days in bed, she was very weak. Claudio was a good man, hospitable, he treated them as best he could with the little food he had. He was careful to prepare chicken broth and vegetables for Andrea. This time they were very lucky, had they not found him she could have died in the woods. Edwards helped him every day, with the small garden he had on the lower part of the valley. The place seemed out of this world, timeless, tucked between the mountains it was like a bubble, where it was never too cold or hot and the clouds flew swiftly overhead driven by a wind that never reached down. Claudio didn't talk much, he used few words to organize tasks and little more. In those days he struck up a friendship with Edwards, despite his appearance as a stiff, city Englishman, with pale skin and hands as smooth as a child's. He had no idea how to work the land, but he was eager and didn't mind getting dirty. One night after dinner when Andrea was sleeping, they went out and sat on the wooden bench by the entrance. The clear sky dotted with stars and the half moon over the hills illuminated them as they drank wine from a bota. Then Claudio recounted that once, when he was young he fell in love with a girl, they married, lived in a small city and although very poor were happy. Soon the woman became pregnant, they both wanted to have many children and a large family. The pregnancy was complicated, she was of delicate health and could no longer work, with Claudio's wages they could barely eat and didn't have enough to pay the rent. Despite her advanced state of pregnancy, the landlord threw them out on the street. A few days later she went into labor, she had caught cold from sleeping outdoors and had a fever, the doctor refused to tend them. Claudio gave his word to pay all expenses in installments, but there was no way, without money there was no doctor. The nurse sent them to the convent. He carried his sick wife in his arms, crossing the entire city while people looked away so as not to see, no one helped them. The nuns took her in at the door and he had to wait outside, he waited for many long hours, then came the terrible news: Neither woman nor child had survived...

It was early morning and you could feel autumn's arrival in the cold air. The three of them looked at each other in silence.

"Thank you so much for everything Claudio." - Andrea said goodbye to him with a tight embrace and two kisses. Before she could continue thanking him, he interrupted.

"I've put goat cheese and fruit for you, though I know girl you don't like it much... I hope you have very good luck." - He held out his hand to Edwards, but the Englishman approached and gave him a strong hug.

Under a purple sky Andrea and Edwards walked away along the small path leaving the valley, leaving Claudio and his small world behind. A part of that place they would always carry in their hearts.

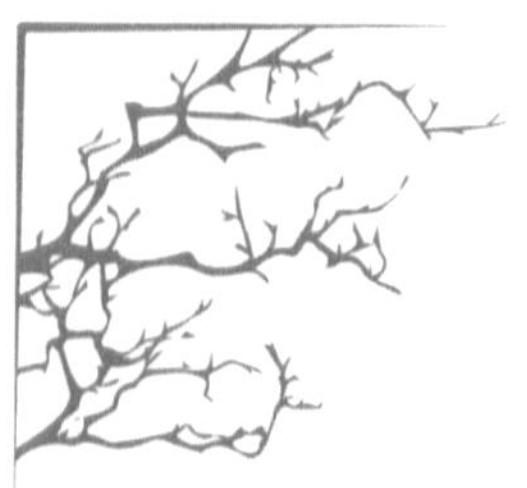

Chapter 13

They were leaving Valencia and entering Cuenca, they had come down from Barcelona through Tarragona and Castellón. The journey had been long, complicated and dangerous, always moving at night, at dawn or dusk and resting during the day. Skirting towns and highways. They didn't have much left, if all went well they would reach Toledo in a few days. They had rationed well the provisions old Claudio had given them. They had been walking for just over two hours since sunset, through arid terrain, white gypsum earth and small shrubs, with scarce trees. They were going down a steep slope, carefully not to fall due to the loose gravel and pebbles on the path. The night's silence was usually interrupted by the song of nocturnal birds. Passing through a crossroads, they heard the nearby hooting of a little owl, then rustling in the bushes and out of the darkness a group of six guerrillas appeared. This time there were no questions, just shoving, until they reached the foothills, where there was a small encampment. The somber faces of those men seemed marked by disappointment, struck by the harsh reality: The young man who voluntarily enlists, with the idea of living an adventure, going to the front, firing a few shots and coming home a hero. What they didn't expect was for the war to last so long, that intelligence or courage didn't protect you from bombs, or machine guns. That the bullets you shoot come back... Those Republican soldiers had seen what a machine gun does to a human body.

After reporting to command, they received orders to move them. They were certain the Englishman was a spy, but didn't know exactly which side he worked for. Apparently there was already information about them. They were put in separate vehicles. Andrea saw through the rear window of the car how they forced Edwards with shoves until subduing him and sitting him in the back of a truck. Then despite the blows he stood up and shouted:

"We'll meet in Toledo!" - A soldier knocked him down with the butt of his rifle to the stomach.

She knew at that moment it was the last time she'd see him. She also had the certainty that she loved him, she was in love with Edwards.

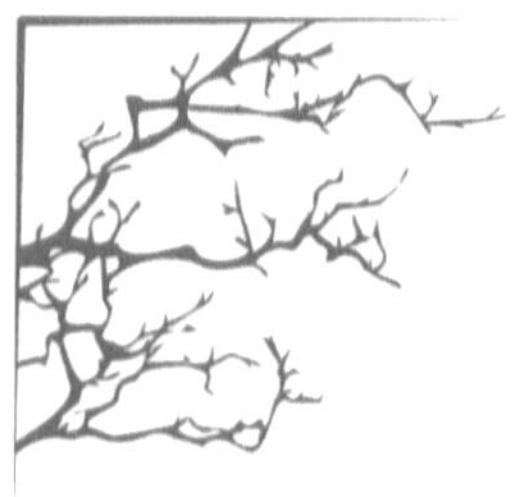

Chapter 14

Present Day

THE WINDOWS OF THE Porsche Cayenne were covered in tiny drops of water, adhering in perfect circular shapes that widened with the drizzle until bursting forming rows dragging several of them from top to bottom. Inside you could hear AC/DC's Thunderstruck. It was a powerful, spacious and comfortable car, plus it didn't draw too much attention. Courtesy of the police department. Some of the vehicles seized from drug traffickers and criminal organizations went to the department for use in various operations. With his sergeant's salary he couldn't afford a vehicle of that type, it was all he could do to pay the bills on the small 600 square foot apartment and the loan on his Seat Ibiza. Jacob activated the windshield wipers revealing number 11 Maqueda Street, near the Campamento metro station in Aluche, Madrid. A group of four very young girls came out of the building. Jacob had a DSLR camera on the passenger seat, with no lens cap, ready to shoot. He took several pictures. They were tall, thin with Slavic features, from Eastern Europe. What was really concerning in this case was their age, too young, it might be a case of underage prostitution. What no one wants to see or talk about in the so-called first world: Abused girls, from families with no resources who get caught by mafia networks. Unscrupulous people who only care about money. Lies upon lies. The promise of traveling to a prosperous country, where once the debt is paid, they can start a new life. Working and studying at the university, finding love and starting a family. But as Sixto Rodriguez says in his song your friends will do it every night. Trying to escape poverty, pushing yourself up by jumping into a black hole.

The four girls entered a nearby call center, chatting casually and laughing occasionally. Jacob could see it through the viewfinder thanks to the zoom on his camera, and imagined their conversations. Upon seeing them enter, he put on some headphones, connected to his laptop. He had microphones installed in some of the phone booths. That same morning, he had strategically placed them while talking to the clerk about Mexican cuisine. He introduced himself as a city inspector, to check the facilities, the fire extinguishers and such. Then he gave him a USB drive so he could take a look at the new regulations on the computer. When connecting the flash drive to the central computer, it installed a Trojan horse that would allow him to access it from his laptop via the WiFi router. Now, comfortably, he could listen to and see practically every conversation. A software program instantly translated the conversations, then at the station, an expert reviewed the conversations in front of a translator.

Polina was the first to enter one of the booths to call her family. The first thing she did when speaking to her mother was ask about her little brother Oleksarder's condition.

"How is Olek, has his fever gone down yet?" - she was worried, she could only call home once a week and since last Monday, didn't know if her brother had recovered.

"He's outside playing, he's a strong boy... How are you?" - The tone of the question was different, her even voice didn't disguise the pain.

"I'm fine mom, don't worry about me. Did you get that?" - She was referring to a money transfer.

"Yes, just this morning. But you didn't have to send so much, you need to save for university, you know."

"It's Olek's birthday this week and I promised I'd get him a bike. Use the money for food and whatever's left over, take him to the store so he can pick out the bicycle. And hide the money well, don't let father touch a cent."

Polina's father was an alcoholic, didn't work and dedicated himself exclusively to spending any money he got on drinking, then he'd come home drunk, always in a bad mood, arguing with his wife and beating her every so often. Since she was a little girl Polina had seen her drunk father come home a thousand times, insulting everyone and accusing her mother of being a bad woman. Since she was little she enjoyed going to school, there she felt safe and dreamed of studying and becoming a schoolteacher someday. There were certain things her family didn't discuss, things they preferred not to acknowledge. No one said a word about her father's drinking and smoking since the age of eight or nine, he learned to smoke and drink before he learned to read and write. About the abuse of his wife and children, nothing was ever mentioned either. Shortly after starting high school, Polina noticed the change in her father's attitude, the strange way he looked at her. One night he came home at two in the morning, drunk as usual. Polina woke up when she heard the sound of her door opening, she turned on the bedside lamp and found her father with his pants and underwear down to his knees. She began screaming hysterically and fortunately that time nothing worse happened, but from that moment on she knew she had to get out of that house as soon as possible. Working for the mafia as an escort girl or staying home, going hungry and being raped by her own father.

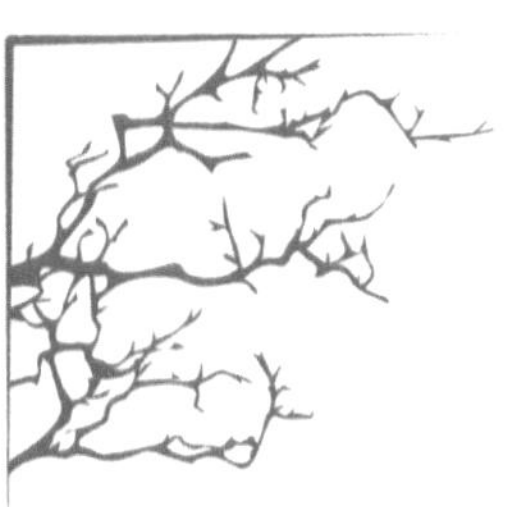

Chapter 15

Sergeant Jacob headed towards the crowd gathering in an area of Calle Carretas. A uniformed police officer shouted for onlookers to clear the area and pushing them back opened up a gap in the crowd allowing him through. Jacob lowered his head as he lifted the plastic police tape. He was used to it, if it's possible for someone to get used to seeing corpses. People who hung themselves or cut their wrists and those who jump off balconies or windows. Suicide cases had increased exponentially with the crisis. Also murders within families, men who killed their partners and mothers who ended the lives of their children before taking their own. Dramatically bloodstained scenes. Working without empathizing, observing and taking notes, without thinking about the story behind it. Something that was practically impossible, to carry out the investigation you had to put names to each body, find out the causes and motives. The medical examiner could get his hands covered in blood by sticking his arms up to the elbows into a corpse's entrails to perform the autopsy, but he didn't need to give them a name. Dead meat, veins, arteries, heart, lungs and everything else. Parts and pieces of a machine. He could rummage around inside like a watchmaker tinkering with the gears of a clock. Jacob on the other hand, had to bring them to life, delve into their past with the help of witnesses, family and friends, until reaching the present moment, reconstruct what happened to deduce how they ended up amidst so much blood.

On the sidewalk, in a reddish brown semi-coagulated puddle, lay a dead young woman, with her neck slit side to side by an extremely sharp object, perhaps a straight razor. A deep cut that had severed her carotid artery and jugular vein. He moved closer and the figure seemed familiar, upon observing her face he confirmed it was one of the young girls from the underage prostitution case he was investigating. Polina, an almost childlike girl, pale skin, black hair and very light colored eyes. He remembered her laughing as she walked with her friends who were talking about something funny. Now her gaze was not the same, the bright light had disappeared and her eyes seemed cloudy, frozen like frosted ice.

Maybe it was her age, but every day the blood affected him more, he felt his stomach shrink, pressure rising to his throat. Unintentionally he put himself in the victim's place. Just yesterday that young and beautiful girl had her whole life ahead of her: Plans to go to London to study after paying off her debt. Since she was little she dreamed of being a teacher at a school. To escape from hell. An abusive alcoholic father who took advantage of her, hunger, cold. Misery. The promise of starting a new life in Spain. Going deeper into hell. Spending long winter nights on the street half naked, being used, licked, slobbered over by rotten toothed old mouths. Beatings by pimps to shake off the cold and sleepiness. All to end up thrown on the ground, throat slashed open. Not even the light of the brightest stars can escape a black hole. No one escapes hell.

He looked around for any clues. The bloodstained latex gloves of the doctor and paramedics from the SAMUR ambulance crew who arrived first. The mobile ICU was parked on the sidewalk, doors wide open and emergency lights flashing. There were bloody handprints everywhere, from the doctors who had tried in vain to save Polina and shoe prints. The characteristic marks left by the treads of police and medical staff work boots. Intense at first then increasingly lighter until disappearing several meters from the corpse. On the sidewalk floor, near where the girl's head lay, under a sea of footsteps, he thought he saw a geometric shape. Someone had drawn a small spiral with their fingers wet with blood. The murderer's signature. The mafias liked to leave that kind of message. Maybe the girl refused to work. Every so often, they sacrificed a sheep from the flock, to warn the others of the consequences if they refused to work or tried to escape. Jacob took pictures of the marks, then the medical examiner ordered the body be removed. A police officer struggled to push back the onlookers crowding the police tape. A few meters to the right of the commotion, a woman's figure caught Jacob's attention. She seemed separate from the rest of the people, as if haloed in light. She wore a white blouse and cream colored tailored long pants at her waist. Very light brown hair almost blonde, styled in a bun, side part and bangs falling over her right eyelid. A few strands had come loose from the hairdo falling in waves to her shoulders. Light, naturally arched eyebrows. She had a lively gaze, blue-grey colored.

The hair stood up on his body and in his memory, although unable to identify the young woman the feeling was familiar, as if he knew her. He left what he was doing and went closer to get a better look. At that moment the crowd jostled violently with all the shoving, from those in the back rows who wanted to poke their heads out at all costs to see what had happened. The officer in charge of crowd control called for order again and when calm returned, she was no longer there, she had disappeared as if by magic.

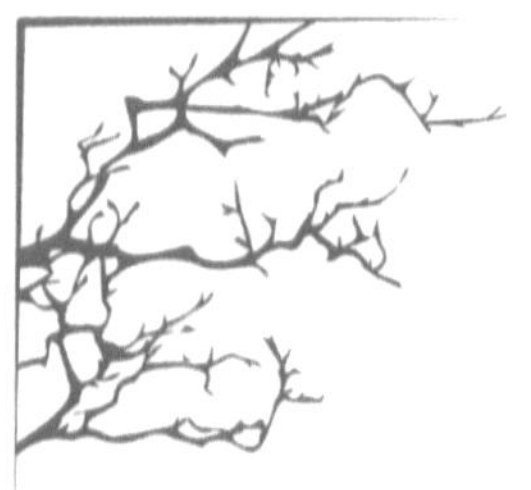

Chapter 16

He logged in entering his password on the laptop into the photo archive from recent murder cases and selected all the images with similar symbols. He found several recent cases. They weren't elaborate illustrations, just very simple sketches made with the victims' fingers and blood. They were reminiscent of the first drawings made in caves by humanity.

It was late, almost one in the morning and he still hadn't eaten dinner. He made himself a sandwich with whole wheat bread, cheese and ham. He sat back down on the couch in front of the laptop. He took a quick bite and drank a swig of beer while scrolling down the image search page. Surprised by one of the photos he saw, when he swallowed the drink it went down the wrong pipe, straight into his lung. The coughing fit nearly made him vomit, when it passed, his eyes were teary and blurry. The image had enlarged on the computer screen. It was a murder on Calle Carretas, a young prostitute killed. The black and white newspaper images from 1936 were practically identical to the ones Jacob had taken that very day. The same place and identical scene, the blood stains seemed analogous. He searched for more information on the old event. A journalist had written about strange drawings painted in blood on the ground. Jacob considered the possibility that it was the same criminal, but the eighty years between the cases made it impossible, even if he had committed the first murder around twenty years old, today he would be over a hundred. The most likely thing therefore, was that just as he had found those images, so had the murderer. Maybe a copycat of old crimes. He emailed the cybercrime department, to see if it was possible to compile a list of people who had searched the Internet for information on that crime. As he clicked send on the email, the window behind with the old newspaper photo popped into full screen, then among the crowd of people, the onlookers behind the police cordon, he saw the image of the same strange woman. He felt an electric jolt. It wasn't possible, it must be some kind of automatic mental association, his imagination. The old photograph was very poor quality and you could barely make out the facial features in the blurry faces, but she was dressed exactly the same. To calm himself down, he thought perhaps it wasn't mere coincidence, it could be a photomontage. The murderer knew the police would look for related images and information and may have placed her deliberately for him to find. The twisted game of an unbalanced mind.

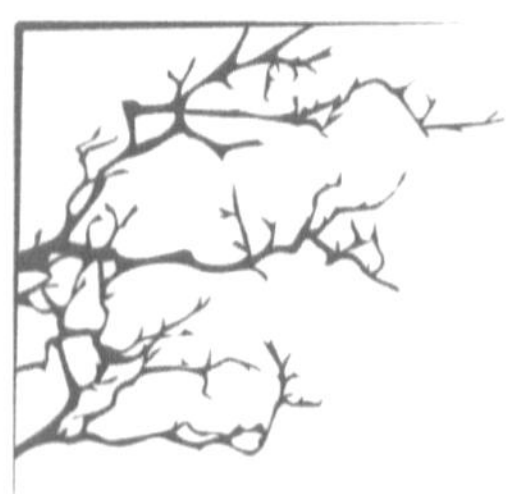

Chapter 17

The front door of the building was open, it was made of thick wrought iron but someone had pushed it with such force that the electric lock burst. Jacob took the elevator and after pressing the button for the ninth floor, waited almost a minute until the battered electronic brain gave the order to go up. There was a jolt and unpleasant metallic sounds, metal on metal that made you inevitably think of the height, falling and being crushed between a pile of junk and debris. He breathed a sigh of relief when he got out, headed to door four and as he reached out his hand to ring the bell he heard voices inside. Foul language and all kinds of insults, it sounded like an argument getting out of hand, although you could only hear Anastasio's voice, Miguel's father. Sergeant Jacob decided to visit his old childhood friend Miguel, who had been released two weeks earlier. A minor drug trafficking matter, retail marijuana and some pills. Normal in the neighborhood and sometimes the only way to survive, although lately even the drug dealer business was in crisis: the young people who didn't have money for pot mixed tranquilizers, anxiety and antidepressant pills with alcohol, some even snorted glue and solvents. The fastest route to escape their problems, misery, at least momentarily.

Miguel and Jacob, two boys who grew up in the same neighborhood and went to the same schools, had chosen opposite paths. Certainly choosing is not the right word; most ghetto kids were predestined from birth. The sergeant knew it very well, unlike his friend, he had opportunities thanks to his parents' help. The politicians who dictate the laws, the rules, live in another world, they come to visit every four years to ask for votes. To save the city by locking up young delinquents in jail, inaugurate another retirement home and promise them higher pensions.

The only things in Miguel's fridge were four beers, a bottle of cheap wine and a jar of pickled onions. As a child before having his blood drawn the doctor asked if he'd eaten anything and he said he'd had some little onions in vinegar at six in the morning. His father never worried about having anything more to eat, not even a carton of milk and some bread slices for breakfast.

He wore old hand-me-down clothes from relatives and friends. He was never bought school books, he had to ask the kids from the year above for their old ones. The last days of class, while everyone was thinking about summer break, Miguel took the chance to ask for textbooks.

He spent entire summers roaming around the neighborhood. In the urban asphalt heat of the Madrid streets. In the Aluche and Carabanchel area, jumping the fence of the municipal swimming pool, on the hottest days. Without seeing the beach until he was 18 years old, when he went with some friends in a stolen car.

Anastasio claimed to be a left-wing revolutionary, a true communist, he didn't believe in the capitalist system. That's why he never bought anything for his wife or son.

"Celebrating birthdays is for dumb kids. Christmas gifts are for dumb kids" - That's what he used to tell Miguel. "Don't call me dad, that's for dumb kids..."

And this was said by a man, who called his parents mommy and daddy, who at fifty were still giving him birthday and Christmas gifts. His mother had always made his bed and gotten up at dawn, to prepare his breakfast before he left for work.

A bottomless pit, everything was swallowed up and in the end it consumed his wife. After years of struggle, she fell into a deep depression, stopped leaving the house and talking to people. Anastasio didn't give her money, claiming the pension was his, that he had earned it with sweat. That's how he understood marriage, all the rights for the man and all the obligations for the woman. She was servant at home, cleaner, cook, mother, twenty-four hour babysitter. While he spent his life at the bar and when he came home drunk, he spat on the floor, pissed on the walls and insulted her. Anastasio refused to buy food and when he saw his wife getting sicker from anemia he laughed. He was extremely frugal watching what others spent. He turned off his son's light even when he was studying or the TV for his wife in the middle of a movie. He refused to buy a measly space heater. They had to spend the winter wrapped in blankets and shower with cold water. She was already very weak, the neighbor came by practically every day that winter and brought her some broth or soup, in the coldest part of winter she gave her an old radiator they didn't use since getting central heating. When Anastasio came up drunk as usual, he was furious.

"I have no teeth because of you and your son's dog. I have no money for the dentist and you're going to waste my salary on electricity..." His face dark purplish red from alcohol and rage.

That same day he threw the radiator in the trash. He made around three thousand euros a month, some even twice as much, plus he had the apartment on Maqueda Street rented out. He also did fake invoices for construction companies for work he didn't do, they offered him an eight or even ten percent cut of the total amount falsely billed. He didn't spend a penny on his home, or give his wife or son a single euro. He was capable of drinking away six thousand euros in fifteen days. Then crying he went to his parents and siblings so they'd lend him more money, claiming his wife and son were starving. Relatives and friends took pity on the poor man and every month gave him something. Money that immediately ended up in the bar.

That winter, a few days later pneumonia finished off the frail woman. Anastasio cried rivers at the funeral, begging his family for help. Softening their hearts and loosening their purse strings. His intention was to get more money to party.

Anastasio wasn't a murderer, he didn't shoot you dead. He looks at you and laughs while watching you starve to death. He laughed the same at the malnourished African children on TV as at his own wife and son.

Many young people in the neighborhood were going through great hardship and even hunger. Going to social services to recount their misfortunes and ending up in tears didn't help at all. It always ended with the following words: Your father should feed you, that's what he gets a pension and two apartments for...

In other words: Fend for yourself.

Start from zero, even worse, to continue living in his house and not end up under a bridge, Miguel had to take care of his father, when the police called him to come pick him up the times he drank every last drop from bars and shops in the neighborhood. They found him passed out unconscious anywhere, lying in the middle of the road blocking traffic. The world turned upside down, all the obligations for the children and none for the parents. When I see an elderly person alone in a nursing home, with no visits from children or family, I wonder what kind of life they must have given them.

Speculating, how most men his age had bought affordable apartments and sold them for exorbitant prices to the young people of his son's generation. Forcing them to go into debt for life, forty or fifty years mortgaged to the bank. The only way to try to leave home, become independent and make their own lives. Then with the crisis and lack of work, they couldn't make the payments, their apartments were taken and the debt remained. Many young couples broke up having to move back in with their parents.

Even prostitution had changed, professionals no longer worked nights near the clubs, now they looked for clients in parks, in the petanque playing area.

In addition to the apartment where he lived, Anastasio had bought another as an investment, when they had a reasonable price and with a construction worker's salary you could pay it off in four years. It was his wife's idea of course, if it were up to him, he would have invested it all in the bar. He's been renting that apartment for over thirty years, multiplying the investment and obtaining twenty times its value. Recently in times of crisis, people couldn't pay such high rents, so rather than lower prices, many decided to keep apartments vacant. A drinking buddy finding out he had that empty apartment, proposed a business deal. He would put up the money to buy some girls.

"It's up to you, but don't fill my place with darkies..." Although he said it aloud, he yelled it in his ear, slurring and spitting in his face.

"No, of course, I bring quality girls, Africans can be bought for three thousand euros and Eastern Europeans go for five thousand, six thousand if they're really young."

"That's the main thing, for them to be very young. And I take care of testing them out when they're new." - He showed his few remaining teeth laughing.

They were talking about human trafficking, about buying girls like livestock. Girls who travel with the idea of reaching a better country, where they can work and study at university. Of course they knew what they were coming for. But they thought they could pay off the debt to the mafia quickly, pay the five or six thousand euros and be free. But that's where the trap was, the debt increased every day. They also offered them drugs, to get them hooked. When they realized they'd been deceived, they'd spent several years prostituting themselves and if they left they put their own lives at risk as well as their families, parents and siblings, who were controlled by the mafia in their home countries. They were condemned to a life of sexual slavery, beatings and abuse.

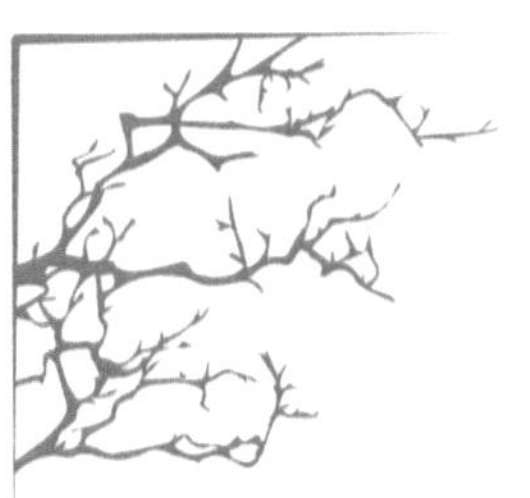

Chapter 18

He barely recognized his friend Miguel, his gaze had changed, now it seemed distant, lost and dimmed behind a dark veil. He said he was fine, but his words weren't believable. Jacob didn't know what he could do to help him. The young man eager to take on the world, with whom he had lived a thousand and one adventures, was gone, no longer there. Over time the rain and wind erased every trace, leaving no trail behind. Jacob feared getting lost in that maze forever. Crossing invisible lines, separating man from beast. With his job, he had to stay alert at all times, because the option of taking the fast route, of taking justice into his own hands, was always within reach. The repeat offender, the abuser or rapist who laughs when caught, aware that with a good lawyer, the judge will release him that same day. The sergeant asked himself over and over if the right thing was to do nothing, knowing that setting him free allows the abuse, rape and murder of innocents to continue. Having the power to put an end to it in his hands. That was one of the issues tormenting him day and night. No one knows what is right or wrong. The criminal plays with an advantage, as he has all the time in the world to plan his crime, carry it out looking for legal loopholes that allow him to escape unpunished.

Miguel got up and stood looking at Jacob, then began to speak. First dryly, then more fervently and passionately.

"The struggle of a lost generation. The inner war... some say." - He gestured effusively. "Try harder... study more... work more... Our parents had life all planned out: study until sixteen, job, girlfriend, military service, get married and have children, steady job, new car and apartment. Our generation didn't have any chance; Forget about girlfriends they told us, what you have to do is study and work, forget about getting married and having a family, think about that after you graduate... How are you going to buy a new car or a house? What you have to do is finish university... Be entrepreneurial, invest all your time and money in the business... take another course get another master's... and before we realized it we were 40 years old. A whole life of effort, learning things that are useless now. We have nothing, empty pockets, neither wife nor children and our minds broken, turned to mush from so much pressure and so many formulas, rules and laws we have to memorize.

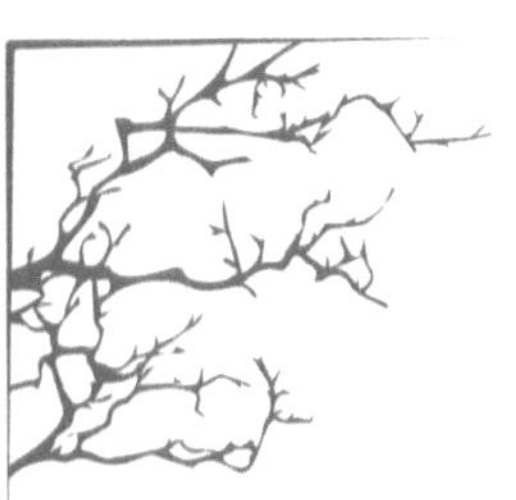

Chapter 19

Thanks to assistance from Hitler and Mussolini, Franco's troops crossed from Africa to the peninsula by means of an airlift. They advanced rapidly through the western half toward Madrid. A quick attack on the capital could have ended the war in a short time. But instead of continuing on to Madrid, they turned toward Toledo. They say Hitler himself personally ordered the liberation of the Alcázar. To this day there is still speculation about that decision. Why didn't they continue on to Madrid? Toledo had no strategic value. Of course, there is no record of what the Nazis were looking for. It's known they were searching for the Holy Grail in Spain, that they returned after the civil war to Montserrat, but no one thought the meaning of the cup was the transmission of wisdom and therefore it was more likely tablets of inscribed clay, parchment or more recently bound sheets of a book.

CAPTAIN ANTONIO MONTECILLOS' company was the first to enter the small town of Piedra Blanca in the Sierra. A small village, less than two thousand inhabitants. Santos García, the school teacher, remained tied to a chair, hands behind the backrest and legs bound to the legs. A thick trail of blood ran from his nostrils bordering the corner of his lips and dripping from his chin.

"Let's just get this over with, I only need a few names... You know, I have to give my superiors something..." Captain Montecillos wiped the sweat from his forehead with a white linen handkerchief. He waited silently, but within seconds his pale face was turning red with anger.

While wiping his brow again, he made a slight sideward nod at the teacher. A large, enormous man, dark skinned with a thick black beard, sweat soaked military uniform of a regular soldier, threw a punch into his right side, straight to the liver. Then he remained smiling, happy like a dog who's brought its master the stick and eagerly waits for it to be thrown again. The pain in teacher Santos García's side was so intense he thought he'd pass out; he would have if not for the bucket of cold water the Neanderthal dumped over him, following Captain Antonio Montecillos' instructions. All of that was unnecessary, there were informants galore. Squealers who switched sides, taking advantage of the circumstances for personal gain. Many denounced family, neighbors and friends. This way they neatly resolved, or rather with a bullet, any grudge. Matters of adjoining lands, unpaid jobs, debts and jealousies. The last was done for free, even paying: "Just make sure they screw over so-and-so... I'll screw myself over."

THE HUGE FIST, SQUARE fingers covered in hair, solid as a rock, punched the teacher's face again knocking out two teeth. Blood splattered the sweaty forehead of the captain, who frowned disapprovingly at the tormentor as he cleaned the fluids diluted in sweat with his handkerchief. The hulking man slightly hid his smile, he knew despite appearances the captain enjoyed it, others' suffering. Santos García's fate was sealed from the start, whether he collaborated or not. When Antonio Montecillos tired of the game, he would shoot him in the temple with his pistol. At times even the living proof that Neanderthals had survived extinction, the half human half ape man, was surprised by the intense evil with which Captain Montecillos acted. Addressing the condemned with friendly words and promises that nothing would happen to them. Giving them false hopes, keeping them alive for hours, days or weeks. Even earning their friendship, only to later execute their own families before them. On one occasion he ordered the tormentor to untie the prisoner, told him he could go home and as soon as he turned his back, shot him in the nape of the neck.

"And you stand there doing nothing? If I don't shoot him he'll get away..." - He said to the giant, while the dead body on the floor convulsed from the spasms.

Teacher Santos García was a man of steadfast principles. He knew full well nothing can be done, said or negotiated with people like Montecillos. It's possible this kind of person never feels remorse, or any fear for the evils and wickedness carried out over an entire lifetime. They are capable of having a wife, children and even going to Mass every Sunday. The cowardly child, unable to fit in among his peers who takes out his frustration hitting younger children in the schoolyard. The atheist who believes in nothing, because he thinks no one is more worthy than him to be called God or the Catholic who sincerely believes he is the Son of God himself, not just any son, he believes he is Jesus Christ himself.

He had his uniform jacket over the chair back, he sat facing Santos. Light green shirt, sleeves rolled up several turns and barely noticeable small splatters of blood. He wore the pants buttoned under his potbelly and held up with suspenders crossing in back trapping the sweat moisture. He was over fifty and his military career had stalled at the rank of captain. Classmates had become colonels and generals.

The barn was dimly lit, some light came in through a small window overlooking the yard, from which came the clucking of chickens. Farm tools and implements were lined up against the walls. In the center face to face sat Antonio and Santos, the other remained at a distance, standing in a corner, enveloped in darkness. The small rectangle of light shone on teacher Santos García's bare feet, which had been smashed with a hammer, bursting nails, flesh and bones. Montecillos took out a cigarette pack from his pocket, put one in his nicotine stained yellow teeth. He lit it with a match and smiling he offered it to Santos placing it between his bloodied lips. After allowing him two drags and realizing things wouldn't progress any further, he took out his pistol and that's where it ended for teacher Santos García.

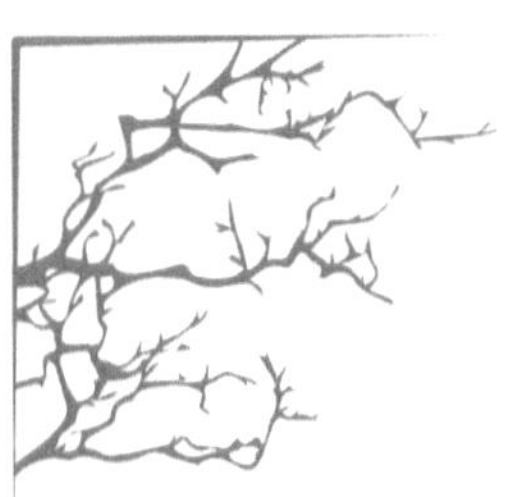

Chapter 20

At nineteen, María Morte was already a very independent woman, she studied at university and after finishing her second year, decided to do some touring, visiting Madrid. In May she spent several days going around the city, monuments, museums and attending plays, concerts and other cultural activities. She had an aunt on her mother's side living in the capital, married with children a bit younger than her. She usually went out accompanied by her fifteen year old cousin Laura. Since Toledo was nearby and buses went back and forth every day, she wanted to take the chance to see it. This time she went alone, caught the first bus very early and by nine in the morning she was already in the historic center area. She walked the small cobblestone streets going up and down the steep slopes. The day was especially hot for the time of year, summer sunshine. She sat on a stone bench in the shade of a tree. Then she saw a young man pass by and upon looking at him, remembered running into him several times. During the minutes she sat in the shade resting, the handsome boy passed three times looking at her without saying anything. That confirmed the encounters weren't coincidental. She waited a bit longer and soon he crossed again. María smiled at him and waved, Felipe got very nervous, he waved back hastily while quickening his pace to get away as soon as possible, but he was unable to stop looking at her, he tripped on the uneven cobblestones and nearly fell on his face, luckily he regained his balance and nothing serious happened. His blushing cheeks were visible from a distance, María held back laughter, she didn't want to be rude.

The tourists and people strolling the streets simply vanished, when she returned to the bus stop she didn't find anyone. She waited with the schedule in hand, but nothing happened. An elderly woman dressed in black with a shawl of the same color covering her head approached and told her not to stay on the street.

THE MORNING WAS SUNNY, a cool, humid breeze smelling of rushes rose from the nearby bank of the Tagus. The sky was clear without a trace of clouds. The singing of goldfinches, canaries and small robins was silenced by the erratic rifle shots heard on both sides of the barricades. The infantry, cavalry and quartermaster academy, Toledo's Alcázar, was under siege by some five thousand five hundred militiamen positioned behind sandbags in the streets, in the inclined roadside ditches and in trenches. Inside the Toledo garrison, reinforced by the civil guard and a hundred civilians in revolt against the republican government. A woman dressed in the typical militiaman attire, overalls with a belt at the waist, rolled up blue shirt, espadrilles and a rifle in her hands, moved in a crouch, carefully keeping her head from poking up over the rows of sandbags and cobblestones ripped up from the streets. She passed behind soldiers, men and women, some uniformed, others civilian, corduroy pants, white shirts and black berets. Farmers, shepherds, bricklayers and shopkeepers who in their free time went up to the high part of Toledo and with a rifle in hand did their part, their quota of shots at the Alcázar's walls.

Andrea de Medina approached a girl who leaning on some sandbags aimed her rifle at the small windows.

"María, news has arrived from your family." - Andrea handed her a letter and the hazelnut colored eyes of the girl seemed even larger.

She was small and slight, barely weighing fifty kilos. Straight hair to her shoulders, chestnut brown, parted to one side with a white headband ribbon tied on the left side. White wool sweater with short sleeves in seed stitch, worn gray wool pants with holes in the knees and esparto grass espadrilles. María Morte with an Italian father and Spanish mother, had family in Zaragoza and the war had caught her by surprise on a tourist trip to Toledo, during summer break after finishing the school year at university. It was the first news she'd had from her parents. She put the rifle on the ground and gave her a happy hug. Sitting back leaning against the sandbags, she nervously opened the envelope. The date was from twenty days earlier, still she was glad to read they were fine. It was practically impossible to communicate from one zone to another. That letter had gone a long way, passed through many hands before miraculously reaching Toledo.

A young, handsome soldier approached them, greeted both women and stood there gaping at María, she had an absurd little smile, you could see they liked each other. But although they ran into each other almost every day the most they'd reached was saying hello and good morning.

"Well then?" - She interrupted after an endless silence where the two remained looking at each other enraptured. "What orders do you bring?"

"Yes, yes, sorry, the commander ordered me to find you. They're having a meeting at headquarters." - He got lost again gazing into María's eyes. Andrea nudged him in the shoulder to snap him out of it. "They need you urgently."

The headquarters was theoretically at the town hall, but in practice they met at the tavern across the way.

"What are we waiting for?" - She had to pat him on the shoulder again.

Felipe said a stupid goodbye, shaking María's hand as if she were a man, standing straight with his head poking up over the sandbags. The whistle of a bullet was heard and Andrea yanked him down forcing him to crouch. The comical situation made María laugh. She kept smiling as she watched them move away, running from parapet to parapet.

UPON OPENING THE DOOR of the tavern a cloud of smoke escaped. Although it was early morning, the place was covered in a thick haze produced by tobacco smoke, indicating planning had gone on a long time, probably meeting since the night before. They were gathered around a billiard table, from which hung a rectangular lamp illuminating the plans and maps they had laid out over it.

"Come here." - Commander Carlos Ávila ordered with a wave of his hand, which also served to disperse the cloud of smoke over the billiard table. "How are things going up there?"

Andrea went over to the table, the commander standing in the center, slightly leaning with his hands on the rail and four other soldiers around him. Commander Ávila's serious face, marked by age with expression lines, briefly lit up when she looked him in the eye, conveying a sense of complicit friendship. He must have been around fifty, short gray hair receding at the temples, white beard and somewhat darker mustache, a color between gray and golden, perhaps tinted by cigarette smoke. His thick dark chestnut eyebrows were well defined, which he tended to move explicitly.

When explaining the procedure, darkness seemed to cover his face, sad eyes, with a special sparkle inside. He looked at Andrea as a father watching a child leave for the front. The plan consisted of digging a tunnel into the Alcázar's walls and using explosives manage to open a hole large enough for a small group to gain access inside. Several soldiers had spent days digging in shifts. They would place the dynamite charge and then she would be in charge of going in and getting the book. Meanwhile they would carry out an intense attack using everything at their disposal, including heavy artillery, to keep them occupied at the other end of the fortification.

"That's all gentlemen." Commander Carlos Ávila gathered the plans and photographs and put them in a folder. The soldiers dispersed, some going into the street others to the bar. "Andrea."

The commander requested:

"Andrea we'll only have one chance. The rebel troops have received orders to liberate the Alcázar. We're out of time."

"No reinforcements will arrive? What about the French and British? What about the Russians?" - Dilated pupils and again like the father trying to safeguard the magic, the mystery of life, in a young child's heart. There will be time enough for disillusionment and distress, to feel life's naked bitterness. When you lose faith, you stop believing in everything; gods, miracles and prophets.

"There are many Nazi sympathizers and good people want to avoid problems. They've left us alone, fighting against Falangists, Nazis and Fascists. Whatever arrives from the Soviet Union, we'll have to pay for in gold.

That kind of talk wasn't common, triumphant speeches were the norm. People thought the war would last four days. That ordinary people with an old rifle or shotgun in hand could beat armies and tyrannical dictators. But wars aren't won with courage and dreams, you need a lot of bullets.

"You'll have to find someone trustworthy. Few people know the reason for our mission. When everything is ready, you'll be in charge of the explosion and going in. I hope that book can change things, maybe we can negotiate by offering it to the British."

WHEN THEY ARRESTED Andrea and Edwards, she was taken to Madrid for interrogation. Usually they didn't go to such lengths with prisoners, but they rightly thought these weren't ordinary people. There was more luck when the person in charge, Commander Ávila, a military man who before joining the army had studied archeology at university and knew the legend of the book, took over. Whether he believed the stories or not, he was informed of the Nazis' interest in getting their hands on it. It wasn't difficult for him to corroborate Andrea's account, her work at the National Library and lack of interest in politics. In a few minutes she went from prisoner to being in charge of preserving cultural heritage. In other words, she would be sent to Toledo on a secret mission, to prevent the rebel troops against the republic from getting the book. He would accompany her himself, to make sure in person that every possible means was being made available.

The last news they had of Edwards was of his disappearance during transfer. Nothing was known either of the soldiers escorting him. It was reasonable to speculate that in all likelihood they had fallen into an ambush and been captured by the nationalist troops. That could not be good, if the Englishman was in the hands of the rebels, he could be tried as a spy and shot at any time. News arrives of the advance of Franco's troops and their interest in reaching Toledo. They had to get into the Alcázar no matter what, they couldn't allow fascists and Nazis to get the book. In Lord Edwards' own words: If they managed it they would start a world war to seize control of all the nations on the planet, imposing a dark regime of terror, a new era, the thousand year Third Reich.

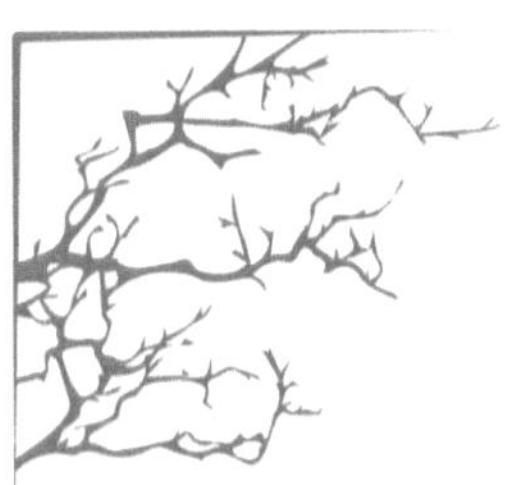

Chapter 21

The shutters on the windows were lowered and a soldier standing guard at the door of the bakery, which was across the street from the western wall of the Alcázar. They entered in pairs, soldiers or militiamen partners, working shifts in the basement coming out smeared in mud and clay.

"I'm telling you it doesn't add up. It won't hold this way... you'll see it ends up collapsing." Pedro said to Paco pointing to the wooden beams.

"Orders are orders..."

"Damn it, but if it collapses it'll crush us, I'm sure the engineer who did the plans won't get caught under it."

The men remained at the tunnel entrance, Pedro shone a flashlight holding it high in his hand. They were covered head to toe in dried yellowish clay. Both were over forty and seemed overweight. Pedro owned the bakery and his belly proved it. There were no holes left in the belt holding up his pants and the buckle about to burst clung to the end by a miracle.

They took long swigs from a wineskin and got back to work. Paco's nose was swollen and bright red. The alcohol thinned his blood making him sweat excessively. Any small task was an effort, huffing as if it were something very heavy or complicated. Pedro lay in the tunnel, using a small hand hoe to dig into the soft, damp earth. Paco crawled in and out over and over, taking out baskets full of mud while placing small wooden planks on the walls and ceiling, following the instructions they'd been given.

"And they said it would barely be noticeable... A tiny little hole... and look what we've done to the bakery... Mud everywhere, sewer stench and if the roof doesn't cave in, the explosion will probably wreck my business." - He grumbled while he worked protesting, Paco paid him no mind, each time he came out he grabbed the wineskin and took a good swig.

The blade of the hoe made a dull thud striking rock. They had reached the stone foundations holding up the Alcázar's walls. He finished uncovering the wall removing the clay with his hands, then the two men left, drank some more wine and informed the boy acting as sentry guarding the door.

That same afternoon, the team made up of Andrea de Medina, María Morte and Felipe, prepared to enter, waiting for the army explosives expert supervised by Pedro and Paco to finish placing the detonating charge. The two argued about the right way to do the job. Neither were explosives experts, they were there despite the orders they'd been given.

"If someone's putting a bomb in my bakery, I want to be there..." Were Pedro's words when the Commander ordered him to stay out of it.

In the north area all the heavy artillery was being deployed, cannons brought from Madrid. So far the Republicans, mostly civilians armed with rifles, hadn't managed to inflict significant damage on the Alcázar's thick stone walls. Pulling back inside when the troops from Madrid arrived, they abandoned the hospital and weapons factory, first taking away three trucks loaded with arms and ammunition. The last one was blown apart by airplanes. Nevertheless, morale inside was weakening, Colonel Moscardó himself wrote to his wife about the ups and downs of depression due to the many difficulties. They tried to maintain discipline among the ranks, but many deserted escaping whenever possible, others couldn't withstand the pressure and committed suicide.

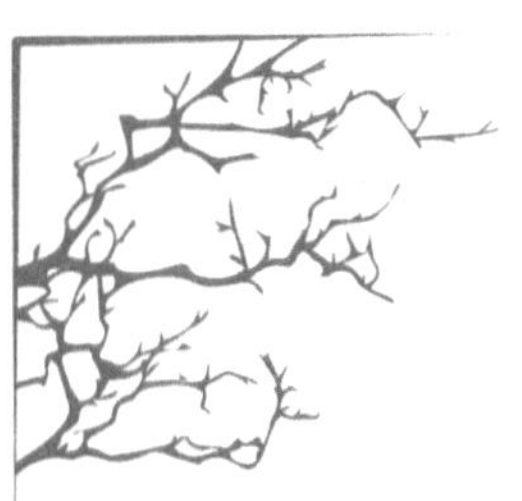

Chapter 22

On September 27, 1936 the Army of Africa led by General José Enrique Varela entered Toledo.

Rifle shots and artillery fire were heard throughout the city. The Army of Africa was entering Toledo. The boy standing guard at the bakery's door ran out toward the nearby command post. The army explosives expert crawled out of the narrow clay tunnel, unrolling a coil of electrical cables.

"It's ready." - He brushed the yellow dust from his pants.

Pedro held the car battery they would use to activate the detonator, running current through the cables by connecting them to the terminals. Meanwhile Paco stood watching, not letting go of the wineskin.

"Well, the moment's arrived, let's take cover and get this over with. Things are getting ugly up there." - Pedro gave instructions as if he were in charge, with the authority conferred by owning the bakery.

The soldier let out cable as he moved toward the corner of the room, where an overturned table on the floor served as a parapet. The street door was kicked in. Two Moroccan soldiers from the regular troops entered the shop, bayonets fixed on their rifles. In the basement, Andrea, María and Felipe took cover behind the table. The weapons were leaning against the wall, around the corner on the other side of the room. Pedro and Paco ran toward them, while the explosives expert kept unrolling the cable wrapped around a stick. Pedro reached the rifle just as the door opened. The only thing Andrea could do was yell to get the attention of the two Moroccans. Those seconds were enough for Pedro to turn toward them taking aim. The intruders fired first, one bullet hit the baker's belly, in turn he shot striking one squarely in the head as he came forward. The soldier collapsed on the floor, as if his legs and the rest of his body were made of rags. The other fired hitting Pedro in the throat. The rifle fell to the floor and he grabbed his neck choking on blood. Paco already had his rifle in hand when another shot was heard striking the explosives expert in the chest, blasting through his heart. Paco missed, the bullet hit the wooden step a few centimeters from the soldier's right foot. Both quickly reloaded their weapons, bolts sliding at top speed. Another deafening boom reverberating in the basement and blood poured from Paco's left thigh to the floor. Andrea watched the scene helpless, she saw Pedro collapse and Paco upon seeing he was out of ammo in his rifle, threw himself on the soldier coming down the stairs, blocking his path. The bayonet pierced his chest coming out his back. To remove it, the African shoved him back with a kick. Paco fell to the floor next to Pedro. María was terrified, crouched behind the table covering her head with her arms. Felipe made an attempt to get up, but as soon as he poked his head out another shot rang out. Luckily the thick wood of the table stopped it. The three were unarmed and the soldier reloaded once more, with a quick bolt action. He had come down the stairs, stepping over Pedro and Paco's corpses, and stood at the tunnel entrance. Without thinking twice, Andrea dove from the left side of the table, grabbing the detonator cable. The soldier yelled something, in another language, but in tenths of seconds Andrea put the cables on the battery terminals and a blast was heard so tremendous it seemed the entire building had collapsed. The bakery basement was filled with dust and smoke. When it cleared, she saw the soldier's corpse, his face and part of his body mangled. The tunnel dug in the earth had created a cannon effect, launching stone fragments with the explosion.

"The wineskin, the wineskin!" - Paco said in a very weak voice, his head resting on his friend Pedro's chest. "Where's the wineskin?"

María Morte went over handing it to him. There was nothing to be done, he was mortally wounded. He tried to lift the wineskin but had no strength, María held it up high while he took a drink. He drank briefly and instantly his heartbeat faded away. The smoke had barely cleared and they had no time to think. More noise was heard upstairs in the bakery.

"Do what you came here to do." - María spoke to Andrea as she picked up one of the rifles leaning against the wall. "We'll hold off the ones upstairs."

Armed they went up the stairs, skirting the corpse of the other dead soldier, while Andrea entered the underground passage with no time for goodbyes, again feeling the bitter sensation that she would never see Felipe or María again.

Outside the fighting was fierce. The troops of Republican soldiers and militiamen wouldn't hold much longer against the Army of Africa's attack.

"We have to keep bombarding the Alcázar's walls with artillery..." - Commander Carlos Ávila, crestfallen, brought his hand to his forehead, aware of the orders he was giving and the sacrifice they entailed.

He moved to the cannon lines at the front himself, to make sure they fired on the stone walls for as long as possible. Gaining some time was the most he could do for Andrea.

Dusk was falling and in the distance you could see the city illuminated by a downpour of mortar fire, flashing with each explosion in a brief flare.

The infantry company led by Captain Antonio Montecillos had entered the historic center area through a breach in the defensive lines. He wasn't there by chance, his intentions weren't heroic, nor of course altruistic. He had relevant top secret information, he knew well why the troops had turned back on their advance toward Madrid. He wasn't going to miss this opportunity. Disobeying the hierarchy and orders received, he moved ahead intending to be the first to get his hands on that book the Nazis coveted so greatly. Once he had it in his hands, he'd think of a way to negotiate a juicy agreement; and he wasn't thinking precisely of a military promotion. He was far more interested in becoming a landowner, a nice estate in the south and maybe some noble title. His company was made up mostly of Moroccan soldiers, only some noncommissioned officers and officers were Spanish. They were tough soldiers with a lot of experience, accustomed to a very different life from ours. Like an assault team, they advanced up the street toward the Alcázar. Two soldiers upon seeing light and hearing noise inside entered a bakery. Captain Montecillos was behind a parapet of sandbags down the street, waiting for his men's signal confirming the way was clear. The hulking giant man, identical to a Neanderthal, stood beside him with the same unwavering expression, absent of any emotional trait. They saw rifle flashes and heard shots mixed with the rest of explosions, mortar shells, artillery shells and thousands of infantry shots heard throughout the city. No one came out of the bakery, so Captain Antonio Montecillos with a wave of his hand ordered two more soldiers to move ahead. The giant abruptly stopped one of them, shoving him back and took his place advancing up the street before entering the bakery.

Felipe peeked his head around the door, trying to see what was happening upstairs in the shop. It was very dark, a bluish light entered through a display window, a storefront showcasing different types of bread. The glass had a hand-painted sign in various colors.

"Wait here, I'll go take a look..." - Felipe whispered in her ear, putting his face very close to her neck and at the same time his soft right hand on her shoulder.

He had never been so close to María and she noticed more intensely the sweet, fresh scent of Marseille soap with lavender flowers. Maybe this wasn't the place or time, but it was possible there wouldn't be any more places or times, she thought turning her head to meet his lips in a fleeting kiss. He turned and with a knot in his stomach walked through the gloom toward the entrance, dodging and bumping into boxes, baskets and other things strewn across the floor, barely visible in the dark. A huge black shadow blocked the light coming through the open door to the street. The human shaped figure raised one of its hands and you could see the gleaming blade of the dagger. Felipe aimed his rifle at the anthropomorphic figure, but before having time to shoot at such close range, he felt a sharp, stabbing pain in his abdomen. His limbs went limp and the weapon slipped from his hands firing as it hit the floor. After the gunshot he felt more pain and more stab wounds, then immediately the pain ceased, blurry vision finally lost in the dark. The young man lay dead on the floor. The tormentor, half animal half man, tormentor of Felipe and so many others, pulled out the dagger embedded in the boy's guts and then wiped the blood from the blade on the corpse's shirtfront. Behind the door, a few meters away was María not knowing what had happened. Felipe's short, muffled shout followed by a gunshot. She was scared to death, but held on to the hope that everything would turn out alright. However remote the possibility. Back against the wall, she took a breath, reloaded her rifle with a quick bolt action and came out aiming into the dark toward the entrance. She saw Felipe's body in the gloom lit by the rectangular light coming through the window in the door. She felt like her heart would jump out of her chest, the suffocating sensation turned to dread from the shock upon seeing the huge, dark figure accompanied by a strong stench of rancid sweat, lunge at her. She felt a strong blow to the head, above her right ear, between the nape and temple. She regained consciousness a few minutes later, feeling intense pain accompanied by ringing in her ears. She was disoriented, didn't know what was happening, it took her several seconds to realize what was going on. The soldier was ripping her clothes off with his hairy paws, while the other held her from behind taking the chance to violently grope her bare breasts as if trying to tear them off. They were about to rape her when Captain Antonio Montecillos appeared coming through the door.

"ANIMALS, LEAVE THE poor girl be!" - He kicked the soldier grabbing María in the behind.

The giant stepped back two paces and withdrew hiding in the shadows, waiting for new orders from his master.

"Are you okay girl?" - He asked worriedly, affectionately, as he approached her to stroke her face.

María broke down crying as she tried to cover her naked breasts with shreds of her torn shirt.

"There, there, take it easy my girl." - He kept stroking her head, as if she were a dog.

While she sobbed, he slowly moved his right hand to the leather holster hanging from his belt over his right thigh. The darkness concealed Captain Montecillos' face, his expression had now changed, he wore a sinister grin as his hand slid slowly like a snake toward María's head with his aimed pistol. He enjoyed watching the innocent girl, who couldn't imagine his evil intentions. Since he was a child his father realized he wasn't normal, he didn't act like other boys. When they sacrificed farm animals, usually chickens and rabbits, Antonio Montecillos didn't just kill them outright. His father did it quickly, mechanically, as if yanking a cabbage from the ground. In an instant he'd snap their necks, without them suffering, but his son took pleasure unnecessarily prolonging the agony. On one occasion his father had to intervene, scolding him and having to finish the job himself, putting the poor dying animal out of its misery. Montecillos strangled the rabbit with his hands and when it was nearly dead he revived it by blowing in its snout, when it returned to life, after taming it for a while by petting it, he grabbed it by the neck again slowly squeezing until choking it once more.

Rows of tears slid down María's face. Antonio seemed to try to console her, but aimed his pistol at the girl's head. He heard noise downstairs and regretfully couldn't continue the charade, he pulled the trigger and María Morte collapsed lifeless on the floor. The captain put away his blood spattered gun in its holster and immediately went downstairs to see what was in the basement.

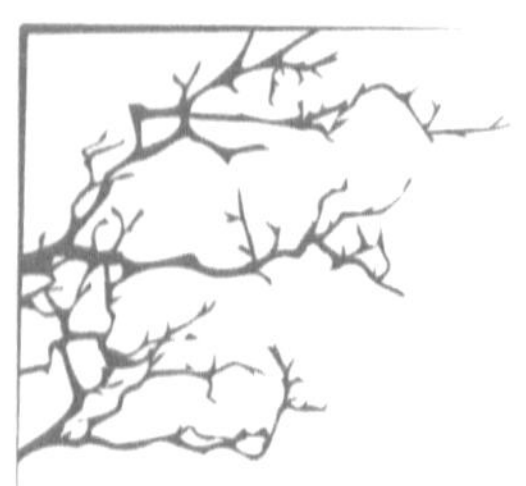

Chapter 23

The Alcázar is located in the high part of Toledo, from where you can see the entire city. Built on solid rock and given its location, since ancient times it was used as a strategic place. Its name comes from the Arabic "Al Quasaba" royal residence, shortened to "Al Qasar" fortress. The building's history goes back to the 3rd century when it was a Roman palace which after the city's reconquest became the praetorium, the magistrate's headquarters. During the Visigothic era King Leovigild established his capital in Toledo in the year 568. Later, during Muslim rule, the works started by Abd al-Rhaman II in 836 and by Ab al Rhaman III in 932 stand out.

Over the years there were continuous expansions, renovations and reconstructions after various fires. Alfonso VI approved an expansion and his successors Alfonso VII, Alfonso VIII did as well. Fernando III greatly improved it and Alfonso X the Wise with the famous Toledo School of Translators, combined the three cultures present in the city: Jewish, Arab and Christian. He ordered construction of the four rectangular towers that form the corners of the building and finished the east façade.

It was a royal residence in the 14th century after the Arab occupation during the Trastámara dynasty. Various interior reforms were carried out during the reigns of Peter I, Henry I, John II, Henry IV and later the Catholic Monarchs who restored the west façade. Subsequently up to the present, each monarch and government has undertaken reforms. It suffered two serious fires that left it practically in ruins. It has had various and diverse uses, and even in the 19th century a telegraph tower was installed, for communication between

Madrid and Cadiz. During the civil war, it was partially reduced to rubble by Republican artillery shells.

WHAT COULD BE MORE important than family, than wife and children? What good is winning a battle or the war, if afterward you have no family or home to return to? Colonel Moscardó pondered inside a besieged Alcázar. He had sacrificed many lives to hold the position, including that of his son, captured by the Republican side and executed after fruitless negotiation. How many lives are a few walls of earth and stone worth? There was no moment doubts didn't arise, the irrationality of it all. If it made no sense at that very moment: What sense could it make years later once the war was over?

The outcome was imminent, from the Alcázar you could see the fierce fighting to take Toledo. That night the downpour of projectiles falling on the walls was far more intense, men and women tried to hold on, fought to contain the countless fires breaking out here and there. It was nearly impossible to maintain military discipline amidst that chaos of people running every which way. The Colonel wondered if it had been worth it or if everything was in vain, the death of so many, including that of his own son.

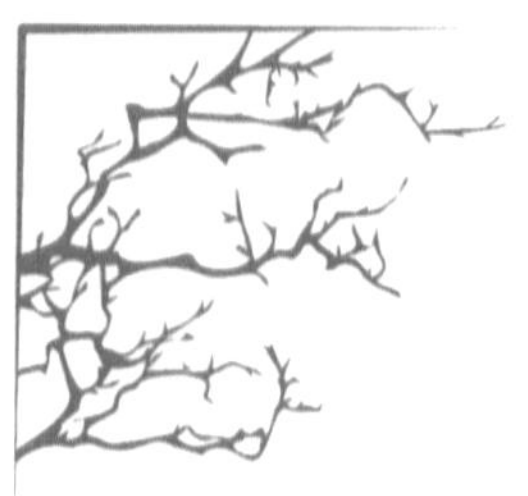

Chapter 24

Captain Antonio Montecillos briefly examined the basement going from one end to the other with slow steps observing everything, he immediately deduced what had happened: The first corpse he encountered on the stairs was one of his men, then he came across Pedro and Paco's bodies, the rubble, the tunnel and the body of his other soldier blown apart by the explosion. He crouched lowering his head to peek inside the hole dug in the floor. He saw a faint light flickering on the other side, the yellowish light of an oil lamp.

Andrea crawled out over the debris dislodged by the explosion. The bombardment the Alcázar was undergoing, directed by Commander Carlos Ávila, was having the intended results. The underground access she had used was deserted, everyone was confronting the downpour of projectiles. The defenders struggling on the north side, civilians, women and children, taking refuge in the deepest basements. She was somewhat dizzy, her vision clouded by the effort of crawling through the tunnel, that and what had happened as well. The tension and fear didn't leave her, she often thought about it, felt unable to go on. She didn't understand where people got the courage, ever since that German came into her house and tried to rape her, she'd had fear in her body. Since that day, she hadn't managed to sleep soundly. Anxiety and suffocation woke her trembling in the middle of the night, sometimes sweating as if she had a fever and others shivering as if hypothermic. She wanted to stop the madness surrounding her, to end it all once and for all, but there was always something forcing her to keep running. An endless race pursued in the dark by her own shadow. Barely a few seconds to catch her breath and she heard the sound of someone crawling through the tunnel. Her heart started pounding erratically again. In the right corner she saw a large wooden barrel, it was empty but very heavy and it took effort for her to tip it over. Then she rolled it pushing with her hands toward the hole. At that moment Captain Antonio Montecillos' head appeared, with his pistol in his right hand and a Pertrix flashlight with pocket watch battery in his left hand. The cellar was lit by the oil lamp, which produced a flickering light as the wick flame swayed. Montecillos shone his flashlight at Andrea. It was the first time they saw each other face to face. He had to duck down quickly putting the top half back in the tunnel, to avoid being crushed by the barrel.

"Communist bitch!" - You could hear him yelling from inside as he banged trying to get out. "You'll see when I get my hands on you!"

She certainly didn't stay there to find out, she grabbed the handle welded to the brass base of the lamp and ran down a narrow arched ceiling passage of reddish bricks. She constantly heard sounds and kept turning to look back, with the feeling of again encountering that man's face. The narrow, dark brick hallway seemed to have no end. A distressing race trying to escape from her pursuer's shots. The light at the end of the tunnel was near but unreachable. She thought of María Morte and Felipe, thinking that perhaps, with a little luck they could escape their captors, unable to imagine they were both already dead. Then she remembered the trip to San Lorenzo de El Escorial, the views of the mountains from the small open top Bentley Sedanca. The fresh breeze laden with the scent of flowers and a warm spring sun shining in the deep blue sky. Then the images returned of the young prostitute dead on the floor, throat slit with all her blood outside her body. Now she remembered it with less distress, barely three months had passed and it seemed like three centuries. From seeing a corpse for the first time, to seeing so many she'd even lost count. War turns the best of people into the worst of animals. The instinct for survival. She had never wished anyone harm.

For Montecillos the situation was different, since the war broke out he did as he pleased giving free rein to his imagination. Behaviors previously shunned and punished with arrests and even jail time were now seen differently. In some cases as heroic acts and in others a necessary evil. Captain Antonio Montecillos once said:

"If you don't like it, don't look, but it's what must be done; what has to be done to win the war. Leave diplomacy to the politicians with their speeches and cheap talk. Afterward we military men are the ones who must get our hands dirty with blood."

Each person justifies their sins as they want or can, but the captain needed no justifications, because he thought he was doing the right thing. Winning battles, keep advancing without looking back, without stopping to count the dead, without quantifying the devastation. A ditch on the outskirts of each town, to bury it all, seal it with sand and quicklime.

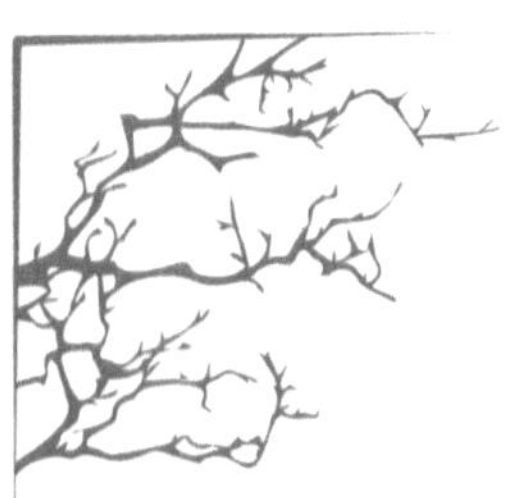

Chapter 25

She finally reached the exit. A rudimentary generator, operated by a belt drive from the rear wheel of a motorcycle, erratically powered the incandescent light bulbs illuminating the Alcázar's interior. She immediately located herself, recognizing the inner courtyard bordered by arches supported on columns of the two levels. They had been informed the book was in the crypt. She had memorized the plans and knew where to go. She saw someone run behind the columns. The figure barely visible under the night sky's irradiation and the deficient electric lighting seemed familiar. He was headed to the underground crypt, it looked like they were both going in the same direction. Following his steps down the corridor, cautiously so as not to be seen, she smelled the characteristic scent of Edwards' perfume.

Shouts, shots and explosions were heard everywhere, the Alcázar's defenders held on as best they could, doing their utmost. They had no reason to think someone could slip through their ranks. Also: who would be crazy enough to go in there? No one would expect a woman like Andrea to sneak in at that moment. If it weren't for the artillery punishment directed by Commander Ávila, it wouldn't have been possible to enter, much less move around inside.

"To the basement, get to the basement!" - A soldier appeared out of nowhere and upon seeing she was a woman told her to take refuge underground.

Andrea was unarmed, when the soldier who materialized from thin air ran toward her, she held her breath, thought she'd been discovered, but the young man was in a big hurry. He had orders to hold his defense post. Shooting his rifle from the assigned window. The boy's face looked like a child, he couldn't be more than seventeen or eighteen years old. He only had time to fire once, then was struck head-on by a projectile. Andrea saw him lifeless instantly, covered in dust and debris from the explosion. A shrill ringing sounded in her ears. She looked toward the crypt entrance and once again, fleetingly saw the Englishman's silhouette. She ran with all her might and upon entering the chapel, shouted his name, but no one was there, just empty pews, hundreds of candles burned down to the base and wax stalactites hanging down. He wasn't there and she thought it was all a product of fear, exhaustion and her imagination, although she could identify his perfume mixed with the melted wax. At the back of the small room was a Christ carving. The wall seemed solid, built of granite, but under the feet of the crucified Jesus, the flagstones had given way from the explosions. It was a false wall covering a passage with walls and steps chiseled into the stone, descending into darkness. She took one of the candles still burning and without thinking twice, entered the passage. She had the premonition this was the right place to hide the book. She had learned from Edwards about the manuscript's relationship with the Catholic religion since ancient times and the secrecy with which the monks had kept it for centuries.

THE VAULTED CHAMBER carved into the rock appeared covered in engravings, from the floor, crossing the ceiling from one side to the other. Roman and early Christian symbols. In the center of the room was a granite tomb, with a life-size figure of a bearded man wearing a crown, a king holding a scroll in his hands. Andrea knew the roll of paper depicted, although different in form, was the same text, the same book. She brushed her right hand over the headstone, dragging away the layer of dust accumulated over centuries and could translate the Latin:

Here lies King Recceswinth.

Bearer of the sacred scriptures.

The Visigoth King Recceswinth 649-672 before ascending to the throne, convened an assembly of clergy and nobles at the 8th Council of Toledo, to repeal the law that obligated him as king to never pardon those who conspired against the crown, condemning to death those who did not pledge allegiance. The council decided the monarch had the final word, the power of god's grace. At the same conclave, the laws of succession to the throne were legislated: Properties acquired during the reign would not be inherited by his children, they would pass to the next monarch, successor to the crown, who would be named by the council of nobles.

At the beginning of his reign in 652 the Basques led by noble Froya who wanted to usurp the throne, rebelled, making a bloody raid, reducing to ashes the populations located on the banks of the Ebro and slitting the throats of all inhabitants. They went so far as besieging the city of Zaragoza, which they finally failed to take. Shortly after Froya was captured, taken prisoner and beheaded. Instead of invoking the ancient law and going to war with the Basques, King Recceswinth pardoned them in exchange for an oath of allegiance. Froya's rebellion was the only armed conflict in the twenty-three years of his reign. Never before in Visigoth history had such a long period of peace been known.

He was also famous for the merging of Goths and Hispano-Romans into one nation. Compiling and consolidating the legislation in force called the Liber Iudiciorum, composed of twelve volumes.

SHE INEVITABLY IMAGINED the people who made the crypt with hammer and chisel. To think of the quantity of centuries passed and how little men have changed. Since forming the first communities, we've always been at war. To think the land belongs to us and the inherent human selfishness leads us to fight and die over imaginary lines marked on the ground. In Spain, we know a lot about this, every town, every region has its borders and we've been warring since the beginning of time. Andrea felt she belonged neither here nor there, to neither one side nor the other and in the end wound up fighting, taking up arms to survive, to defend her life. She wasn't the only one, most fought on the side they were dealt and not the one they chose.

She slowly circled the tomb, examining every detail and discovered a different area on one of the bases. One of the shields wasn't carved into the rock, it was a piece of terra cotta that seemed added on. She tapped it lightly with a closed fist as if knocking on a door. It produced the expected sound, the piece served as a cover, sealing a cavity. She was completely focused on translating the engravings and finally getting to the bottom of the mystery. Suddenly like an electric shock, she felt a presence right behind her. She turned around instantly and barely saw Antonio Montecillos' face, felt a strong blow to her left cheek with such force it made her lose her balance and fall to her knees. The blow near her ear caused vertigo, and the floor seemed to move like a boat on a choppy sea, then came the pain and later the feeling of fear, upon finally understanding her situation. Montecillos made a smiling grimace placing the gun barrel at Andrea's temple. He said nothing, simply pulled the trigger. She closed her eyes and thought this was the end, but all that was heard was a metallic click. The gun was empty, Antonio had used up all his bullets fruitlessly shooting in the basement. She heard Ernesto's voice again giving instructions as if he were in the corner of a boxing ring. She lunged at the man's knees knocking him down forcefully. The captain was bewildered, his back hit the floor violently, he felt a sharp pain in his neck, but reacted immediately throwing punches at the woman pouncing on him. Andrea struggled, tried to block the blows raining down while throwing her own. Despite his superior position, it wasn't a fair fight. She barely weighed a hundred pounds, while Montecillos was nearing two hundred. Although she shielded her face keeping her arms raised in a defensive boxing stance, the punches exploded against her head, spinning it from side to side. One of them squarely struck her temple, leaving her semi-conscious, a situation Antonio Montecillos quickly took advantage of to get her in a chokehold with his arm around her neck, a choke preventing her from breathing, strangling her. The candle left on the stone tomb was about to burn out completely and go out. The flame's struggle to stay alive was analogous to Andrea's fight to breathe. Her heart struggled fruitlessly to send blood to her brain. In an instant everything went black. In her final moments, Andrea de Medina recalled a familiar scene, when her parents were young and her brother Ernesto a child, they all laughed happily that summer day picnicking under a grove of trees by the riverbank. Time flowed slowly driven by the current of crystalline water sparkling under the sunlight like thousands of tiny mirrors.

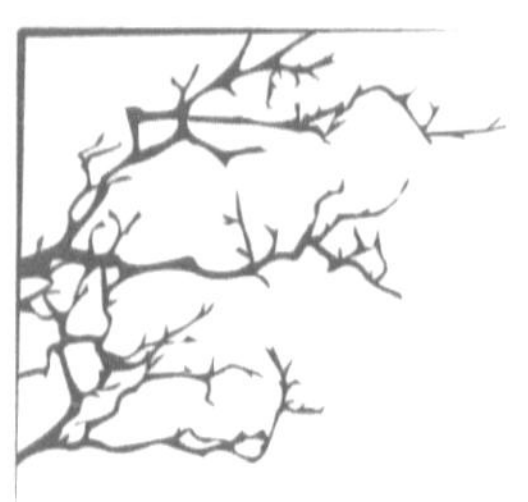

Chapter 26

Since the murder of young Polina, Jacob had the house on Calle Maqueda under 24 hour surveillance, with special monitoring of Polina's three female housemates. He knew their names and also had a lot of personal information about each of them. Iryna was the oldest, but also the most innocent and ignorant, she was a redhead, very freckled and had grown up on a farm near a small village, among sheep, cows and pigs. She was the least sociable. Katerina was the tallest and gangliest, looking like a basketball player. Yelyzaveta looked like a boy, with very short hair parted to one side and very muscular. She was also the one most concerned about the state of her companions, despite her physical appearance she was very kindhearted and always joking around to cheer up the other girls. All with their little box full of broken crystal dreams.

Sergeant Jacob patrolled one of the areas where the young prostitutes were forced to ply their trade. He went through the African zone, divided into different ethnicities and countries, then the Latin and Latin American zone, and finally found the street with the Eastern European girls. And he grimly pondered what he was seeing: The meat markets had prospered in recent years. Women of all races, from any part of the world, grouped by nationality in parks and industrial areas. Every so-called first world country fed these mafias. And we're capable of calling ourselves civilized men. Risking your life crossing the Mediterranean Sea to end up here, on the foul smelling streets of an industrial park, making partial friends for twenty euros and full service for thirty. That's how we help the poor of the third world, putting them on all fours.

IT WAS GETTING DARK and Jacob got out of the car where they did their stakeouts for a moment. His legs were numb from sitting so long, when he stood up his knees cracked, he discreetly stretched near the vehicle, wearing large dark sunglasses and a baseball cap so as not to be recognized, but upon looking down the street, he identified Anastasio, Miguel's father, so as not to be discovered, he casually turned his back, as if looking at the other side of the sidewalk. Anastasio entered the building, that seemed like a strange coincidence to him. The apartment where the girls lived was in a woman's name, when they gave him the report he didn't notice, it was the information for Miguel's deceased mother, Anastasio's wife. He didn't make any changes in the registry to avoid having to declare it and avoid taxes.

He muted the music player in the car and rolled down his window, impulsively in a movement induced by his subconscious. The night brought a cool breeze entering through the window. The first woman's scream he heard was a short, dry cry of terror, then came another longer one of muffled pain, stifled by hands trying to silence it. Jacob came running out of the vehicle toward the nearby entrance, while with his right hand he checked the weight and feel of his black neoprene shoulder bag, where he carried his service weapon. Anastasio still hadn't left the building, so images immediately came to the police sergeant's mind of what could be happening inside.

"Shit!" - He punched the elevator door and upon confirming it was out of service, kicked it and ran up the stairs.

The amber colored reinforced glass windows, which were supposed to let in street light, were bricked over from the inside. Jacob pressed the light switch on the first floor, but the circuit breakers had been ripped out and when he touched the bare wires he felt the electric shock. He let out four curse words and kept running up the deteriorated entrance hall practically in the dark. Smoky ceiling and walls from tobacco smoke and the floor covered in paint flakes falling off.

The apartment door was ajar. Now the screams had ceased and nothing could be heard inside. He carefully opened it and immediately came upon the unpleasant scene. In the living-dining room there was broken glass everywhere and the white textured walls were splattered with blood. On the floor lay the body of one of the girls. He immediately identified her, it was Iryna, the very freckled redhead. He checked for a pulse, placing his index and middle fingers on her neck. They had hit her on the head several times with a blunt object, a steel bar, hammer or wrench. Her heart had stopped, he'd arrived too late.

The naked light bulb hanging from the ceiling swung back and forth, the dim lighting gave the feel of being in a ship's cabin battered by a storm. He wiped the blood from his hand on the denim of his pants, while feeling a mix of rage and sorrow for not having arrived in time. He heard footsteps on the other side of the door leading to the bedrooms. That alerted him and then he sensed the presence of the two girls hiding behind the sofa. They were crouched, terrified by what had just happened. Jacob kept calm and pressed his lips with his index finger in a sign for the girls to remain silent. Now he cautiously stood up, taking out his Heckler and Koch USP "Universelle Selbstladepistole." Universal self-loading pistol in German. A USP Compact 40 with 13 rounds of 9mm ammo. The solid feel of the cold metal and the weight in his hand immediately gave him greater confidence. He approached trying to make minimum noise, avoiding stepping on the broken glass. He didn't know who would be on the other side of the door, or if they were armed, so he slowly turned the knob opening it carefully. The hallway was dark and the swaying light from the dining room illuminated it at times. Something came running out of the shadows, giving him no time to react. Anastasio charged him like a bull, knocking him on his ass. When he was in firing position

Miguel's father had already escaped running down the entrance stairs. While running in the dark going down the stairs he called headquarters on his cell, for them to send a patrol car and ambulance to Calle Maqueda.

"Stop right there!" - He shouted upon exiting the building. "Police, halt!"

But Anastasio was thirty or forty meters away and paid him no mind, instead he ran faster. Sergeant Jacob felt a twinge under his left pectoral due to the stitch in his side. How was it possible? He asked himself: The man he was chasing was practically an old man, a retiree and moreover he knew for sure his habits weren't at all healthy. He ate the tapas they served him at bars, pig's ear, tripe, chorizo and blood sausage, all saturated fats, the pork offal sold at the butcher shop. He'd smoked two or three packs of cigarettes a day since he was ten years old and since that same age he hadn't touched water. It was a mystery, a true medical paradox. Anastasio should have died from cancer over thirty years ago, but not even cancer wanted to go near that man.

The apartment where Miguel and his father lived was two blocks further ahead. The police sergeant saw him enter the building. Then a woman walking briskly also went into the entrance, the electric light from the streetlamps gave her hair the color of liquid gold. Although she had her back turned, he recognized her figure, it was the young woman he'd seen in the crowd on Calle Carretas and who later appeared in the old scanned images uploaded to the internet from 1936 newspapers.

The elevators were stopped, going up in one would be like stepping into a death trap, he had no choice but to climb the nine floors by stairs. He trained at the gym every day, still he was short of breath and felt faint, kept at bay by the nervous tension of the situation. Once again, the apartment door was wide open, this time gaping open, showing the small hallway and dining room. All the interior lights were on. He entered in assault stance, arms extended aiming forward with the gun prepared to open fire if necessary. A foul, nauseating stench reached deep into his lungs, leaving him nearly breathless and gritting his teeth to keep from retching. The kitchen to the right and dining room in front, both places packed with plates of rotten leftovers and piles of crushed cigarette butts on them. It wasn't the typical spoiled food smell, it was more a bittersweet mix: vomit, sweat, rotten meat and cigarette butts. Dead dogs on the roadside, colonized by fly eggs and devoured by a ravenous swarm of voracious larvae. He moved across the living room toward the back of the house, the silence and apparent calm gave him chills. This time he was alert, he wouldn't let himself be caught by surprise again. He reached the main bedroom and to his surprise found Anastasio lying on his back on the double bed, with a kitchen knife stabbed in his chest. A quick, precise stab to the heart, so recent there hadn't even been time for blood to appear. That threw Jacob off, up to now he'd had it all neatly tied up, a solid case. Anastasio and his connection to the murdered girls, outstanding accounts, the pimp and his sex slaves. But now he didn't know what to think.

"You really don't remember anything?" - He barely recognized Miguel's voice, it seemed broken, serious and calm. Too calm

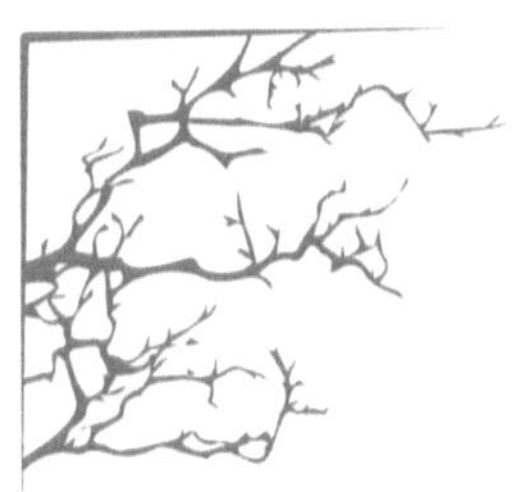

Chapter 27

Upon waking up dizzy, he felt for the first time the pain from the blow to his head. When he fell unconscious to the floor, he seemed to hear his friend Miguel repeating several times: "She is mine, She is only mine...". But he had no idea what he was referring to.

Old, forgotten memories came to Jacob's mind, like the old slideshow presentations they used to do in school. He had the key to his parents' house, the old family home where he had lived until becoming independent at twenty-four. Since his father's passing three years ago, the house had remained practically empty, his mother had lived in the village since then, with one of her also widowed sisters. It smelled closed up and dusty, the blinds completely lowered and utilities shut off. He opened the main electrical panel of the house and switched on the breakers, then turned on the lights and went upstairs where the bedrooms were located. His room was just as he'd left it, exactly the same. A teenager's room, with posters of his favorite band AC/DC on the walls and a balsa wood model airplane hanging from the ceiling. He went straight to the bed and from underneath began taking out clear plastic boxes, full of memories: comic books, cassette tapes, old issues of Rolling Stone magazine and finally he found what he was looking for. An old book bound in brown leather. Until that moment, he didn't remember anything, the pact and all that had been forgotten, as if it were part of a dream or an old movie. Now he was certain everything that happened had been real. He remembered the day he was in the old church square with his friend Miguel, the priest's library and how he took the book hiding it under his shirt. Then images came to him of the cemetery.

If he put together the pieces of the puzzle, his friend Miguel fit perfectly. Places and victims he surely knew about. The timeline was correct, the murders began when he got out of jail. But why?

The book opened to the exact page where the old incantation appeared, the one they had unsuccessfully recited that summer so many years ago it seemed an eternity had passed. He heard the creaking of the wooden steps, someone coming upstairs. The footsteps stopped on the other side of the door, the golden knob turned and Miguel appeared. His very curly black hair was streaked with white strands. His small, black, distrustful and aggressive eyes recalled those of a sewer rat.

"You all treat me like a loser. This time will be different. The power of that book will be mine." - He seemed like one of those preachers on channel 33, the ones that come on in the wee hours. He was completely deranged, as if he'd taken some kind of drug.

"But why did you kill those people? Those poor girls weren't to blame for anything." - Jacob kept calm, spoke to him as if they were still old friends. The bag with his gun was on the bed, next to his right leg. "Why them?"

"They were whores..."

Jacob felt a surge of anger. The word he used to describe the girls and the disdain with which he said it infuriated him. He knew everything behind it, we and our civilized society had put them there, working a street corner. No girl chooses to be a whore if she can be a princess. The most beautiful flowers cut down and thrown to the pigs. He remembered Polina's conversations with her mother and how excited she was to be able to give her little brother a bicycle. He also remembered Iryna, with her orange hair and freckled face. They were practically children. Girls born into misery and poverty. Into their own hell.

Now he wasn't looking at him, his eyes were fixed on the book. His eyes wide open nearly bulging out.

"That book belongs to me." - He finally said in a low voice, as if speaking to himself. "I'm the chosen one, Lucifer, the reborn antichrist."

He said the last part aloud, confirming Jacob's worst fears: Miguel had completely lost his mind. Maybe he couldn't handle prison, his mother's death and living with his father, although Anastasio could barely be called that; the most he'd done was have bad sex. On the other hand, there was the question of drug use. The new designer drugs could turn a reasonably normal person into a cannibalistic killer.

He leapt at him in a diving tackle but didn't grab the book, instead he took the black bag where he carried his Compact 40. The zipper was open and the gun fell to the floor. They both lunged for it scuffling. The police sergeant was aware his life depended on it. If Miguel got the pistol, it would all be over. Jacob was stronger, but Miguel seemed possessed by the devil, a rabid dog, he scratched his face and bit his arms. He did a judo hold they'd taught him in the self-defense classes at the police academy. He had him gripped tightly by the neck, squeezing hard, in a few seconds he stopped struggling, his limbs went limp. He didn't want to kill him, only knock him out, manage to subdue him and cuff him, then call for backup at headquarters. Upon loosening the pressure on Miguel's throat, he suddenly thrashed landing a powerful elbow to his face. He cut his right eyebrow open, bleeding profusely. The blow was so blunt and forceful he nearly lost consciousness once more. But he gritted his teeth and took it as best he could. Without letting up an instant he dove for the Compact 40. They both grabbed it at the same time. Then began a struggle for survival. It was a dangerous game, Russian roulette, if the gun slipped from his hands he was a dead man. Somehow Miguel managed to yank it from him in one of the tugs. At that very moment he felt an explosion of energy inside, an intense heat and with all his might headbutted him in the face breaking his nasal septum. Miguel released the gun as he collapsed. The Compact 40 powerfully hit the parquet floor firing the round in the chamber. A flash followed by a boom, then the smell of gunpowder,

Jacob saw he wasn't injured and sighed slightly relieved, but upon looking at his old friend was shocked. The bullet entered through his left eye, grazing the lacrimal bone and exited between the right temporal and parietal, leaving a large hole where his inner fluids spilled out. Part of the brain matter was stuck to the ceiling.

All the light bulbs in the house shone brighter, the room lit up in a blinding white light for a few seconds, then all the bulbs exploded. It seemed like a power surge. The furniture, bookshelves with old science fiction novels, began to vibrate knocking everything they held to the floor. The Star Wars figurines first then the rest. It was the start of an earthquake that gradually gained strength. In moments it was so intense the whole house would collapse. Jacob ran downstairs holding onto the railing and leaning against the walls so as not to lose his balance. Upon going out to the small yard, everything fell into an ominous calm. He realized the entire city was dark, it seemed all the lamps including the streetlights had blown. He had his cell phone in hand and called headquarters, but there was no service. He tried again, this time the emergency number that operated on a different band and barely needed coverage, but got the same result. As soon as he hung up, he felt watched. The feeling was familiar reminding him of the night they summoned the devil at the cemetery. Now those old memories surged strongly, vivid and precise, as if they'd happened yesterday. He looked around the small garden and immediately noticed a human figure staring at him fixedly from the shadows.

"Police, come out of there right now." - That was the first thing that occurred to him, but when that being moved toward him, he wasn't so sure he'd used the right words.

The figure approached the area lit by the stars and moonlight. The celestial bodies shone in the sky with an intensity he'd never seen before. The shadow took female form and to his surprise he saw it was the mysterious woman.

Andrea de Medina's now very light, bright blue eyes observed him. Jacob gestured not fully grasping what was happening. He had the last piece of the puzzle in his hands but resisted putting it together.

"You called me first saying my name then reciting the incantation. You opened the doors to another dimension." - He remembered reading the name written in pencil on the endpapers of the book and then reciting the invocation.

"Are you the Devil?" - The sergeant's words came out with difficulty, stuttering. Andrea who looked exactly the same physically as the morning in 1936 when he found the book, as if time hadn't passed for her, smiled upon hearing that.

"Angels and demons are merely a simple way to explain something very complex. Good and evil... but none of that exists. Only parallel dimensions, things we can't see or hear, beyond our comprehension. A tangled skein crossing and intertwining: space and time. We live eternally, we're born, we die and are reborn, repeating the same mistakes over and over. The most atrocious, bloodthirsty demons aren't locked up in hell; they're flesh and blood men living among us. Wolves in sheep's clothing..."

"But the book..." - He vaguely appealed.

"The book is merely the physical representation of the forbidden, the unknown. An apple in paradise. Confronting our own fears. What people refuse to see looking the other way. But we wanted to know, to understand how the universe works."

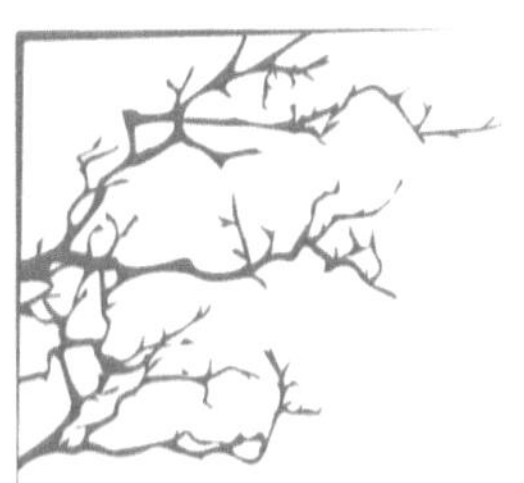

Chapter 28

Antonio Montecillos wrapped his arm around her neck in a closing lock that prevented her from breathing, strangling her. The candle left on the stone tomb was about to burn out and go off completely. The flame's struggle to stay alive was analogous to Andrea's to breathe. Her heart struggled unsuccessfully to send blood to her brain. In an instant everything went black. In her last moments, Andrea de Medina remembered a familiar scene, when her parents were young and her brother Ernesto a child, all laughing happily that summer day having a snack under a grove by the river. Time flowed slowly driven by the current of crystalline water that sparkled under the sun's rays like thousands of small mirrors. All her fears and anxieties completely disappeared. The calm after the storm and rest at last leaving behind so much suffering. But the pain returned, the creaking of the vertebrae in her neck about to burst. She felt a strong blow and the tomb room lit up with a bright, dazzling light. Again she smelled the musk of the Englishman, but this time when she finally managed to focus her blurred vision on the figure in front of her, as the fog cleared she saw him. Lord Edwards looked at her with his unwavering smile. Next to him was the body of Captain Antonio Montecillos, with his skull caved in on one side by the blunt blow of some object. Andrea de Medina deduced what had happened, it was clear that the Englishman had arrived at the right time. He crouched in front of her, then stared at her. Andrea was still stunned and without saying anything she threw herself into his arms.

The captain's corpse with its eyes open and twisted mouth with tongue sticking out, seemed to laugh at his own death. A mocking grimace. A tragicomic end for a little man who had done so much harm and caused so much pain to so many people.

While she remained tightly embraced to the Englishman, sudden flashes came to her memory, in a distorted movie of distorted images and sounds that began to clear up in increasingly clearer and sharper sequences. He began to speak, in such a way that he seemed to read her thoughts. His voice with its characteristic accent sounded rhythmic, just as a father's voice sounds when he reads a story to his son.

-"Remember what you were doing the day we first met at the National Library. You had just received some boxes with very old books... One caught your attention, a book bound in thick leather, with a spiral engraved on the cover. You called me when you read the spell and now you are the bearer. You remember the story I told you about my ancestors. Well I am the young man who went in search of the grail...

Now she could see it clearly, the book had been in her hands from the beginning. She even remembered pencil marking her name and date inside and doing what she had never done before, taking the book home with her. When he appeared she had just read the spell out loud without realizing it and that was when she first saw Lord Edwards. She also remembered the sinister German who chased her to her apartment, the dead girl on Calle Carretas, the blood spilled on the floor, that suffocating feeling and later what happened at her house. Now she knew that the black shadow similar to an animal that had formed in her mind was actually him. Lord Edwards had pushed the Nazi over the balcony. She hardly understood anything, she did not understand the purpose of the trip, of the search. But she supposed that this is how the great mysteries of life must be. So complex that they escape our understanding. Life itself is a meaningless journey, the road to nowhere. What did I gain? I was losing it. And amid so much confusion a small flame finally lit up inside her. An infinite journey into the spiral of time. She closed her eyes and hugged him tightly, pushing her left cheek against the Englishman's chest.

The spiral of time

FROM OUR POINT OF VIEW, time follows an unperturbed line. The count, sum of the clock's steps. One, two, three... yesterday, today and tomorrow. But what if that was only something figurative, the logical way for our brain to order time, hours, days and years? For the worm anything not at ground level does not exist, until the bird that eats it comes flying.

In a country where alcoholism is normal, where there is a tobacconist on every corner and a bar every ten meters, open almost twenty-four hours. Not smoking or drinking sets you apart from the rest of society. I wonder: What breaks the chain? Alcoholic grandparents, drunk father, men of taverns and then suddenly a son who does not understand bulls or football, who starts painting on the walls of the cave...

Haphazard mutations in DNA. A joke from mother nature, perhaps they have deteriorated their genetic code so much with drug abuse, that it has become nonsensical and the deformed son sees the world differently, in another way.

Did you love *Escaping from Hell*? Then you should read *Commander Valentina Smirnova*[1] by Francisco Angulo de Lafuente!

[2]

Commander Valentina Smirnova

In an era when women had no voice or vote and were frowned upon outside of the kitchen, Valentina Smirnova flew her Polikarpov I-16 fighter plane fighting against Franco's Fascists, Mussolini's Fascists and Hitler's Nazis in the skies of war-torn Spain.

Russian snipers. The Nazis were losing their minds over those women.

Lyuba Vinogradova

At the end of this book an explanatory annex has been added, about basic combat flight maneuvers used at that time. The era of propellers, when piston engine aircraft - Hispano-Suiza, Daimler-Benz

---

1. https://books2read.com/u/3yQ7El

2. https://books2read.com/u/3yQ7El

or Rolls-Royce Merlin - dominated the skies. Although this is a historical novel documented on real events, both the plot and characters are fictitious. Some authentic details have been altered according to the needs of the fiction.

Read more at https://twitter.com/Francisco_Ecofa.

Also by Francisco Angulo de Lafuente

Destination Havana
Eco-fuel-FA (ECOFA) A viable solution
El Olfateador нюхальщик
Los Mejores (The Best)
То,что Вы не должны делать ,чтобы стать писателем
◇◇◇◇◇◇◇◇◇ ◇◇◇◇◇◇◇
Compañía Nº12
Destino La Habana - Destination Havana
EL OLFATEADOR
La leyenda de los Tarazashi
LÁZARO RIP
Estrella fugaces en el cielo de verano
Commander Valentina Smirnova
Escapando del Infierno
Comandante Valentina Smirnova
Freak - El Circo de los Horrores
INVADERS La invasión ha comenzado
The Sniffer
Una boda gitana y un funeral escocés
Freak - The Circus of Horrors
Escaping from Hell

Watch for more at https://twitter.com/Francisco_Ecofa.

About the Author

Francisco Angulo Madrid, 1976

Enthusiast of fantasy cinema and literature and a lifelong fan of Isaac Asimov and Stephen King, Angulo starts his literary career by submitting short stories to different contests. At 17 he finishes his first book - a collection of poems – and tries to publish it. Far from feeling intimidated by the discouraging responses from publishers, he decides to push ahead and tries even harder.

In 2006 he published his first novel "The Relic", a science fiction tale that was received with very positive reviews. In 2008 he presented "Ecofa" an essay on biofuels, whereAngulorecounts his experiences in the research project he works on. In 2009 he published "Kira and the Ice Storm".A difficultbut very productive year, in2010 he completed "Eco-fuel-FA",a science book in English. He also worked on several literary projects: "The Best of 2009-2010", "The Legend of Tarazashi 2009-2010", "The Sniffer 2010", "Destination Havana 2010-2011" and "Company No.12".

He currently works as director of research at the Ecofa project. Angulo is the developer of the first 2nd generation biofuel obtained from organic waste fed bacteria. He specialises in environmental issues and science-fiction novels.

His expertise in the scientific field is reflected in the innovations and technological advances he talks about in his books, almost prophesying what lies ahead, as Jules Verne didin his time.

Francisco Angulo Madrid-1976

Gran aficionado al cine y a la literatura fantástica, seguidor de Asimov y de Stephen King, Comienza su andadura literaria presentando relatos cortos a diferentes certámenes. A los 17 años termina su primer libro, un poemario que intenta publicar sin éxito. Lejos de amedrentarse ante las respuestas desalentadoras de las editoriales, decide seguir adelante, trabajando con más ahínco.

Read more at https://twitter.com/Francisco_Ecofa.